nancy rue

'NAMA BEACH HIGH
new girl in town

ZONDERVAN®

GRAND RAPIDS, MICHIGAN 49530

ZONDERVAN.COM
AUTHORTRACKE

www.invertbooks.com

'Nama Beach High Book 1: New Girl in Town
Copyright © 2003 by Youth Specialties

Youth Specialties products, 300 South Pierce Street, El Cajon, CA 92020, are
published by Zondervan, 5300 Patterson Avenue SE, Grand Rapids, MI 49530

Library of Congress Cataloging-in-Publication Data

Rue, Nancy N.
 New girl in town / by Nancy Rue.
    p. cm. — ('Nama Beach High ; bk. 1)
"Zondervan."
Summary: When her family moves from Missouri to Panama City, Florida,
sixteen-year-old Laura Duffy feels as if she will never fit in, but she
joins a newly formed group and, along with the other "misfits," learns
coping skills, self-esteem, and reliance on God from Panama Beach High School
counselor Mrs. Isaacsen.

 ISBN: 978-0-310-24399-1 (pbk.)
 1. Interpersonal relations—Fiction. 2. Self-esteem—Fiction. 3. High
schools—Fiction. 4. Schools—Fiction. 5. Christian life—Fiction. I.
Title. II. Series.
 PZ7.R88515Ne 2004
 [Fic]—dc22

                                                                    2003011382

Editorial and art direction by Rick Marschall
Edited by Karyl Miller
Proofread by Laura Gross
Cover and interior by Proxy
Printed in the United States of America

7 chapter one

17 chapter two

29 chapter three

41 chapter four

53 chapter five

63 chapter six

77 chapter seven

85 chapter eight

93 chapter nine

103 chapter ten

117 chapter eleven

127 chapter twelve

139 chapter thirteen

151 chapter fourteen

163 chapter fifteen

I, Laura Duffy, made a decision on October 20th of my junior year. It was a decision that rocked my world.

After three days at Panama Beach High, it was obvious that I was essentially the biggest loser in Panama City, if not on the planet, and that nobody was ever going to speak to me. Period.

My decision: I couldn't spend another lunch period pretending I didn't CARE that I was being ignored. I knew kids believed being a loser was contagious; I believed it too. I wouldn't want to be friends with me either.

Decision: I was going to go to my locker, get a book, and eat my peanut-butter-and-sweet-pickle sandwich oblivious to all because what I was reading was so utterly stimulating . . .

Okay, so it was still pretending, but at least with a book in my face nobody would see my awkward expression. You know the one people get when they feel like a large second thumb? Eyes darting all over, looking for a place to light. Skin the color of your mother's nail polish. Smile plastered on in an attempt to look perfectly fine with this get-me-OUT-of here situation.

Minus the smile, in my case. I wasn't willing to show the entire student body of Panama Beach my mouth full of sparkling ortho-dontia. I think I was the only sixteen-year-old girl on record who was still in braces. And who didn't have significant breasts to speak of. And who took obsessive care of her contact lenses because she lived in fear that she'd lose them and have to wear her glasses. Glasses as thick as headlight covers.

I made the decision after I walked into the cafeteria that day and dawdled near the doorway, pretending to adjust my backpack—I was becoming the master pretender—and watching groups form at various tables. Granted, these were the people who didn't have cars or weren't friends with people who had cars or didn't have the guts to leave campus even though they weren't juniors or seniors and thus weren't allowed to. Otherwise, they'd be screaming up Highway 231 right now, headed for the mall so they could choke down a Wendy's hamburger while breathing in the delicious aroma of acrylic that wafted out of the nail salon. I'd have given anything to be exposing myself to that kind of damage.

Let's face it. I'd have given anything to be one of the FRESHMEN currently carrying their trays of nasty pizza to a table where obnox-ious friends were waiting to snatch bites, be called retards, and laugh as if that were actually funny.

Isn't that what friendship is all about? I thought.

I couldn't really answer myself. Not that I hadn't had friends at one time. In Missouri, I'd had plenty. I mean, good grief, I'd been in six clubs and was an officer in every one of them. When anybody mentioned "school choir," my name usually came up in the next breath, because what DIDN'T I do in the choir program? And I was pretty much known for my grades. They were sort of legendary, actually. Before me, nobody had ever gotten an "A" in Mr. Polk's Honors Junior English course. Not the first six weeks, anyway.

Yeah, people knew me back at Harry Truman High School. I always had somebody to sit with in the cafeteria. Until my parents ripped me away from it all and brought me here, where I could only WATCH a group of girls lean their heads together over a table until you couldn't tell one streaming mane of long, some-shade-of-blonde hair from the other, and then rear back whinnying in unison over some private—precious—popularity-provoking joke.

That was the actual instant when I made the decision. I couldn't do it another day, another minute. The only thing worse than looking like you were alone and awkward was crying over it for all to see.

I turned so fast my Skechers squealed on the linoleum as I headed for the lockers at a trot. I knew the SROs—those were the security officers but I hadn't figured out what those initials stood for yet; I just knew it wasn't "Standing Room Only"—would write you up for running in the halls, and I personally didn't care at the moment. What I didn't know was that the locker area was strictly off-limits during the lunch period.

You'd think I would have figured it out the minute I rounded the corner and found myself in a completely deserted section of the school. The banks of lockers were eerily silent of the usual clanging doors and muffled swearing and tumbling-out books and subsequent swearing that was NOT so muffled. I was used to having to shove my way through gaps between people that your average mouse couldn't maneuver, but there was absolutely nobody there.

As relieved as I was to be out of the judging eyesight of people who were wondering who the outcast was, I felt a little creeped-out as I went for the next bank of lockers over, where mine was conveniently situated on the bottom of four. You get the leftovers when you don't check in until the second six weeks is already under way.

I should have gotten a clue from that creeped-out feeling and let the sudden attack of heebie-jeebies I was experiencing turn me right around and take me back.

To what? To the slap-in-the-face evidence that I was so lonely, I felt like I was physically dying?

I zoomed around the corner, as fast as the butterflies in my stomach would let me go, and almost ran head-on into two girls who obviously couldn't have cared less about the lockers-during-lunch taboo.

They were standing facing each other, bodies taut as if they were dueling marble statues. One of them was a white girl, the other a black girl. From there, all differences ended. They had the same hard bony frames, identical venomous looks in their eyes, and angry frozen faces. "LET GO!" said one.

"You let go!" said the other. The white girl had the black girl by the ponytail. And the black girl had a vice grip on the white girl's loop earrings and was yanking off her ear lobes. I gasped audibly, which was the last thing I wanted to do because then they both whipped their faces around and looked at me.

I was witnessing my first cat fight; I was so scared, I was sure my next move would be to pee on the floor.

"What are you lookin' at?" White Girl said. Her voice reminded me of gravel going through an aluminum funnel. An image of her smoking her second pack of the day flipped through my mind.

Before I could answer, Black Girl said, "Don't you know you ain't supposed to be back here durin' lunch?"

The appropriate answer would have been, "Don't you?"

But I simply shook my head. I was already hating myself for being such a wimp, but these two were at least a head taller than I was and looked as if they'd had a lot of practice at this fighting thing. Then, of course, there was the operative word, *two*: two of them and one of me. I didn't know how to fight ONE girl, much less a pair of them.

"No, I didn't know," I said. "I just moved here."

"Well move on OUT," Black Girl said.

I was planning to. But the fear of going back to the cafeteria was carved more deeply into me than I'd thought, because these words came out of my mouth, all by themselves: "I will. But I need to get into my locker first."

"So do it," Black Girl said. She gave me a sneer that should have sent me scurrying around the corner like the chicken-slash-rabbit I was.

But I shook my head and said, "You're standing in front of my locker."

Up until then, the only sound that had come out of White Girl was a lot of heavy breathing steaming from flared nostrils. But the second I took a timid step toward my locker, she let go of Black Girl and grabbed ME by the front of my shirt. From someplace far away, I heard my peasant blouse rip, followed by the retreating footsteps of Black Girl.

White Girl didn't appear to miss her. She was too busy slamming me up against the lockers and pinning me to them with her bony hands. Tobacco breath huffed into my face as she said, "You tell anybody you saw us back here fightin' and so help me I will kick your—"

"I won't!" I burst in. "All I wanted to do was get a book out of my locker."

White Girl blinked at me for a moment, still breathing out the smell of stale cigarette smoke. Her hold on my shoulders loosened up slightly, so now I only felt like a few of my ribs were broken, as opposed to all of them AND my sternum.

"Who are you anyway?" she said. "I never saw you before."

"I told you I was new," I said.

"Well, let me just fill you in, New Girl. You don't mess with me. You don't EVER mess with me, OR my boyfriend."

From the close range I was being treated to, I could see that her very blue eyes were bloodshot and puffy like the ones on forty-year-old women I'd seen at the Mini-Mart, buying cartons of Marlboros. Her murky blonde hair was pulled up so tightly into a ponytail, I was surprised it didn't slant those eyes out to her ears. They flashed around us now, as if she'd just discovered that Black Girl was missing. My guess was that she'd "messed" with White Girl's boyfriend.

Oddly, my next thought was, *Even THIS chick has a boyfriend. No wonder everybody thinks I'm a loser.*

It was enough to juice me up. I ducked under White Girl's arms and started to leave.

"I'm not done with you!" she said.

"Well, I'm done with you!" somebody who sounded like me said back. My backpack was sliding off, so I let it drop down and I held it by the loop. All the blood had pumped to my face, and I was breathing every bit as hard as she was. I think I was twice as angry.

This had to be somebody else. Laura Duffy didn't GET angry.

"I said don't mess with me, New Girl!" White Girl said.

The gravel was racing through the funnel. She came at me like she was going into some kind of football tackle, head down, shoulders lowered. I could feel all my energy rushing to my chest, and I swung my backpack into the air and brought it slamming down, right on the back of her head.

It took White Girl to the floor, knees first. I was staring down at her, my backpack still in follow-through, when I heard someone behind me say, "Okay, stop right there. Step away. It's over."

I couldn't "step away." All I could do was look at White Girl and let the color drain out of my face. I suddenly felt pale and cold.

"Come on, it's over," said a female voice.

It was Dr.—oh, what was her name? She was the assistant principal who had registered me last week. All I knew was that she wore Liz Claiborne suits and running shoes and that right now I was in big trouble with her. Her manicured nails dug into me as she took hold of my arms from behind and yanked me back.

Meanwhile, the uniformed SRO, which I much later discovered stands for Student Resource Officer, suddenly appeared out of nowhere. He was huge and had a neck like the hulk. He squatted down and put his hand on White Girl's shoulder.

"You okay, Shayla?" he said. It didn't surprise me—later, when I could actually think again—that he knew her name.

"I will be when you get your grubby hand off me."

The officer stood up and reached a beefy hand down to her. "You want some help?"

"No, I do NOT," she said. She rolled over on her back and pulled herself up to rest on her elbows so she could look at me, where I still stood, firmly in the custody of Dr. Whoever. "What I want is to press charges against HER. You saw her attack me."

"I also saw you goin' after her like a line backer," the officer said. "Let's go. We're goin' to go down to the office and sort this mess out."

He had the slow drawl of the born-on-the-Panhandle people that still sounded to me like a tape being played on a Walkman with almost-dead batteries. But as slow and soupy as his speech was, I could tell he was pretty sick of this whole situation already. I had never been a student that the discipline office got sick of. In fact, it was the one place at my old school where no one had known my name. Right then, I was feeling pretty sick myself.

In fact, as Dr. Whoever escorted me out of the locker area and across the hallway to the office area, I felt the lunch I hadn't eaten coming up.

"I'm going to throw up," I said.

Dr. Whoever looked at me doubtfully from under her carefully tweezed eyebrows. I covered my mouth with my hand, but I was already doing the retching that was going to make that pretty ineffective.

"Go—in there," she said and pushed me in the direction of the girl's restroom. I bolted in and barely made it to a stall before I tossed my cookies, or, in this case, my Rice Krispies.

"Gross," somebody in the next stall said.

"Nas-tee!!" said somebody at the mirrors.

I waited until they were both gone before I emerged, shaking, from the stall and rinsed out my mouth. Against my own better judgment, I looked in the mirror.

Stricken-wide brown eyes looked back at me. My usual dairy-fed, ruddy cheeks were as white as the sink I was leaning against. My sort-of-dark, sort-of-red hair was now wet on both sides of my face from the mouth-rinsing, leaving those pieces straight while the rest still held the crimping I'd spent an hour doing that morning. I'd hoped it might nudge somebody to at least say, "Didn't you know crimping went out in the '80s?"

"Fat chance," I whispered to the unnerved image that looked back at me. "Now you're a punk."

I couldn't stand to look at myself for another minute.

Dr. Whoever was waiting outside, impatiently tapping her Reeboked toe.

"What's your name?" she asked. Her inflection said she had heard it before but it had escaped her.

"Laura Duffy," I reminded her. "I just transferred here from Missouri last Friday. You registered me. I was an Honors and Advanced Placement student but it was too late in your semester to get me into any of your version of that—what you call your 'Math and—'?"

"Our MAPPS. Oh, yes," she said. She looked me full in the face for the first time. "Four-point-oh. I remember now. So, besides studying, you like to fight?"

It wasn't my fault! I wanted to shout at her. But I'd done my share of shouting for the day. Maybe even for the rest of my life, I hoped.

Because whoever that had been who got so angry at the whole entire world in that flash-of-a-second that it took for me to hit Shayla over the head, was somebody else. She wasn't the Laura Duffy I knew.

Dr. Whoever was still giving me curious looks as she ushered me into the dungeon—the detention zone, the discipline office. We went straight through the outer room where six dudes in too-big pants were scattered, and entered an inner office that set me shivering.

They must have had the air conditioner turned up full blast because it was about twenty degrees below zero in there. The cinder block walls and the metal desk where the assistant principal was ensconced didn't help. It was all I could do not to throw myself in front of him and beg for mercy. But I couldn't. I was shaking too hard.

"Take it easy," Dr. Whoever said. "Sit down here."

She nudged me into one of the cold chairs.

That left me six feet away from Shayla, who was sitting next to Mr. SRO, in ready-to-spring position. Her eyes never left my face. I sure hoped SRO Man was watching because I wasn't equipped to defend myself again. I had my backpack, but no anger. Right now, I was just scared spitless.

Dr. Whoever leaned over the desk and murmured something to Mr. Discipline and then left. He glanced at me, bright blue eyes boring into me from beneath perfectly white hair that seemed to have made a premature entrance onto his otherwise young-looking head. The next time I saw him, I wondered if he went to a tanning bed or the beach every day—but not right then. I just closed my eyes and thought, *Please, please, please don't suspend me.*

A vision took shape of him dragging me into a room with one-way glass, then pacing behind me as he shouted accusations, forcing me to collapse, weeping, on the table and confess to everything from the Kennedy assassination on. It was the worst I had ever felt, until the door opened and the female SRO brought Black Girl in. Then I started to cry. Just bawl, right there in front of two police officers, two of the toughest girls on the planet, and a man who could ruin my high school career, not to mention my home life. I covered my mouth so they couldn't hear me choking out sobs.

They're gonna gang up on me, I thought miserably. *I'm the New Girl. They can convince these guys that I just came in there swinging because it's their word, their double word, against mine!*

"What's SHE squawkin' about?" Black Girl said.

"She TRIED to deck me after you split," Shayla said, "and now she's goin' DOWN."

"All right, that's enough out of both of you," Mr. Discipline said. "Keesha, you sit." He looked at me. "Laura Duffy?"

"Yes, sir," I said.

He passed me a box of Kleenex from his desk. "I'm Mr. Stennis. Dr. Vaughn tells me you just recently moved here."

"Yes, sir," I said again. I tried to focus on him, but I was having a hard time not looking up at the ceiling for a naked light bulb.

"You weren't aware of the rule against going into the locker area during lunch?"

"No, sir."

"Did you get a student handbook when you registered?" he said. "I don't know."

He cocked an eyebrow at me that required an explanation.

"I got a whole packet of stuff but I haven't had a chance to look at it yet. I will, though!"

I knew I sounded pathetic, even without the snickers from across the room that were quickly hushed by the two officers. It didn't occur to me then to wonder why both of the SROs were in here, when there were 1500 kids outside just looking for trouble.

"I'd advise it," Mr. Stennis said, "if you want to stay out of trouble."

I could only nod. A new flood of tears was on its way.

"Tell me why you were at your locker, Laura."

"I was getting a book—"

"And I was standin' in front of her locker and she decked me!"

Mr. SRO took hold of Shayla's arm and pulled her back from starting a lunge at me. Even at that, I shrank back into my chair, heart pounding. At least it scared me out of crying.

"You'll get your turn," Mr. Stennis said to Shayla. He turned back to me. "What happened when you got to your locker?"

I forced myself not to look at Shayla and Black Girl, who I knew were boring their eyes into me like power drills. I glued mine to Mr. Stennis's tanned face.

"Shayla and the other girl—"

He pointed toward Black Girl. "Keesh?"

"Keesha," she said coldly.

Without looking I nodded.

"Go on," Mr. Stennis said.

"They were both there and they were fighting. Then they saw me, and Keesha told me to go away, but Shayla grabbed me and pushed me against the locker and Keesha ran away."

"She did not!" Shayla said. "Keesha was there. She seen the whole thing—"

"Give it up, Shayla," Mr. SRO said dryly. "You just said yourself a minute ago that she ran off. Now zip it until it's your turn."

Shayla then made a sound that I know I'll never forget. She hissed, through her teeth, only it had the same threatening spit to it that a cat's hiss does when he's baring his incisors. Ready for the kill. I swallowed hard in an attempt to push down the panic that was rising up my throat. If I ever saw her outside this office, I knew I was toast.

"What happened after Keesha took off?" Mr. Stennis said.

"Shayla told me never to mess with her and when she kinda let go of me a little, I got away from her and picked up my backpack. And then when she came at me, I hit her over the head with it."

"In self-defense," Mr. Stennis said, finishing my sentence.

By now he was half-sitting on the desk, arms folded across his coach-like chest, facing me and nodding. I looked right back at him and told the only lie that came out of me during that entire interrogation.

I said, "Yes."

Mr. Stennis looked at me long and hard with his piercing blue eyes. I just knew he was hearing what was going on in my head, the thoughts all screaming: *It wasn't self-defense! It was rage—and I never felt rage before—and I'm so scared. I'm SO scared!*

He didn't appear to hear them, however, and he turned to Mr. SRO. I guess they had worked together long enough to make words unnecessary, because Mr. Stennis gave a soft grunt and Mr. SRO nodded.

And evidently Shayla had been with the two of them enough times to know the code, because she said, "That AIN'T the way it went down."

She looked at me, eyes spewing venom. I covered my face with my hands and burst into tears. Uncontrollable tears. The kind that make you lose track of where you are until a female SRO has walked you down a hall through hordes of staring students and deposited you in yet another office.

It was the kind of crying that kept me from caring WHO was going to question me now. I just kept sobbing into my hands until I felt a person sitting down in the chair next to me. She smelled of coffee and put off heat like a space heater.

"Just go on and cry it out," she said. Her voice lilted over the words.

I looked up, tears and snot streaming down my face. I didn't know it then, but I was gazing into the face of a woman who was going to change my life. Forever.

chapter two

The woman didn't look at all like she sounded or smelled. She had gray-and-black short hair that looked crispy, as if it would crackle if you touched it, and she had a pair of those half-glasses that I've never understood hanging from a gold chain around her neck like she was afraid they'd run away if she put them down someplace.

She had to be older than my parents—by about ten years—because she was kind of thick around the middle, not fat but just no longer curvy, and she had a white sweater around her shoulders the way nobody but a sort-of-middle-aged woman wore a sweater. Under it was a brown blouse that exactly matched her eyes.

That was about where I stopped taking inventory: her eyes. They were chocolate-colored and small and bright, kind of like a bird's, and they were young. Way young, like Bonnie-my-six-year-old-sister young. I figured out right away what made them that way—there was no judgment in them.

Decision: This was somebody I might be able to trust and I'd better start talking fast, before Shayla and Keesha had Mr. Stennis and the police department talked into placing me under arrest. It was too easy to picture myself being led away in handcuffs to a smelly holding cell full of Shaylas and Keeshas.

"I don't know why I did it," I said. "I've never gotten that mad before! I hardly ever even get mad! Period. But it was like this other person inside me took over and hit her with my backpack. I'm not a bad person. I've never been in trouble like this my whole life. I don't even take two pats of butter!" I put my hands up to my face. "Maybe I'm just going crazy."

"I don't think you're any crazier than the rest of us."

She smiled at me, and the lines that radiated from the corners of her eyes crinkled so deeply I could almost hear them crackling. I sank back into the chair I now realized I was sitting in. It was an easy chair with padded arms. And there was framed art on the walls, prints I knew I'd seen in coffee table books. And there was even a rug over the industrial strength carpet, a deep-pile rug with squares of russet and green and butterscotch all over it.

"You're in the counseling suite," she said. "I'm Mrs. Isaacsen." She chuckled, and it sounded, not surprisingly, like wood cracking under flames.

"I'm Laura Duffy," I said. I'd stopped crying by this time, and I took the Kleenex I was still clinging to and scrubbed under my eyes. That glance in the mirror back in the bathroom had revealed that what little mascara I was allowed to wear was trailing down my cheeks like two black creeks.

"It's nice to meet you, Laura," she said. "I wish it could be under better circumstances."

"They're going to suspend me, aren't they?" I said.

"I doubt it, all things considered."

"What things?"

"Shayla and Keesh."

"Keesha," I said. "Don't call her 'Keesh' or she's liable to deck you."

"Exactly my point." Mrs. Isaacsen smiled wryly. "This isn't the first time either one of them has been hauled in for fighting, not by a long shot. But this may be the first time they've had a witness who was willing to tell the truth. Sounds like you were pretty brave in there."

"Brave? I was scared to death. I'm surprised I didn't wet my pants!" I looked down at my carpenter jeans, the ones I loved. "I didn't, did I?"

Mrs. Isaacsen didn't even blink her wonderful eyes. "Not that I know of," she said. "Though I have known students to do that very thing when faced with Shayla. I don't think Mr. Stennis is considering any consequences for you. Sort of an exchange for your willing testimony. He'll probably call it self-defense and let it go at that."

I looked down at my lap again and rubbed the tops of my thighs with my palms. Only then did I see the rip right down the front of my favorite peasant blouse.

"You want a sweater to cover that up?" Mrs. Isaacsen said.

I tried not to rivet my eyes to HER sweater when I said, "No thanks."

She nodded slowly. "I think maybe we ought to send you home anyway. You've had a pretty traumatic experience."

"I lied when I said it was self-defense," I said to my lap.

She barely hesitated. "Because you feel like you attacked her when you could have just run," she said.

I nodded. "I'm so weirded out. I've never lost control of myself like that before, ever."

"Never ever?" Mrs. Isaacsen said. "You've never slammed your bedroom door when your parents ticked you off? You've never hung up on somebody who was being stupid on the phone?"

"No!" I said. "I'd get grounded so fast."

Mrs. Isaacsen leaned back in her chair and crossed her legs. She was wearing khakis and brown flats, one of which she let fall off at the heel as she swung her hanging leg back and forth.

"So you like to be in control of yourself."

"Yeah," I said. I twisted my lips for a second. "It's not like I can control anything else."

"That bad, huh?"

That was all she had to say. That and the kindness in her brown eyes had me spilling my guts about the move and all I'd left behind and all the emptiness here. I was ready to cry again by the end.

She passed me the Kleenex and said, "I hate it for you."

I stared at her in mid-nose-blow. "You aren't going to tell me that this is a tremendous opportunity for me to meet new people and make new friends?"

"It may be," she said, "but it's also about the hardest thing you'll ever do in your life. I love teenagers—otherwise I wouldn't be here—but for a bunch of people who complain about adults being narrow-minded, they can sure shut doors in people's faces, especially if they don't know them."

I really did start to cry then. It wasn't the headed-for-the-mental-hospital kind of bawling I'd done earlier. These were tears of relief. So far, she was the only adult who had understood what I was feeling. You have to cry when something like that happens.

"I can see I'm going to have to stock up on my Kleenex if you and I are going to spend time together," Mrs. Isaacsen said.

"Are we?" I said. "I mean, am I emotionally flipped out or something?"

"No, darlin'," she said. Southern women, I'd learned, used pet names as easily as most of us use *and*, *or*, and *the*. It slid off her tongue like a floating feather. "No, SHAYLA is 'emotionally flipped out.' You are simply reacting in a normal way to an abnormal situation. But it can become more normal for you, and I'd like to help you through that process, if you're willing."

I got anxious. If she was going to suggest counseling or therapy or whatever they call it, my PARENTS were going to be emotionally flipped out. We Duffys didn't talk about our stuff outside the family. We didn't even talk about our stuff INSIDE the family. Unless somebody from the school called them, Mom and Dad were never going to know what had just happened to me.

"What I have in mind," Mrs. Isaacsen said, "is a group that's going to meet during the activity period on Tuesdays and Thursdays. You wouldn't be the new girl in there because it's just starting, and I don't think any of the girls I've invited know each other, at least not well. It's a big school."

"Yeah, I noticed," I said ruefully.

"Will you consider it?" she said. "You don't have to give me an answer right now. Sometime before Tuesday will be fine. I'll save you a spot."

I was actually tempted to give her a "yes" right then. It wasn't like I HAD any activities to go to during activity period. The day before, I'd hung out in the library and tried to do some homework, only there were a bunch of other people in there who evidently didn't have activities either, nor did they want to. What they wanted was a place to plan their OUTSIDE activities, which as far as I could gather were tantalizing the cops at the mall, finding a rave, and scraping up enough money to rent a room at the Motel 6 so they could "Par-teee!" It wasn't hard to pick all of that up, since they were all ignoring the librarian's finger-to-the-lips and glares in their direction. Being in a therapy group had to be better than that.

But that was just it. Therapy. Why did I suddenly need that? I hadn't been the one to decide to move away from the place where

I'd lived for sixteen years. If we were back in Missouri, none of this would have happened.

"Give yourself time to think about it," Mrs. Isaacsen said. "There's no pressure here and there will be no pressure in the group. If you come to a couple of meetings and you hate it, you can bail out. Fair enough?"

Her eyebrows went up into little upside-down V's, like exclamation points over her dancing eyes. I had to nod.

"Fair enough," I said.

I looked at the clock on her desk, which was shaped like a frog's head. The hands on it were two very long tongues.

"Has fifth period already started?" I said. "I can't miss chemistry or I'll be so lost."

"That was the only MAPPS class they could get you into, huh?" Mrs. Isaacsen said. "That's a shame. All your classes should be advanced placement. Next semester, I'm sure we can get you in, after people take their semester finals and start dropping out like flies."

"Yeah," I said. I didn't add, *Wonderful. I'll be the new kid all over again*, although that was what I was thinking.

Not that my new-kid status was going to change much between now and the middle of January anyway. At this rate, I was sure I'd still be walking around trying not to look like No Name. I should have felt relieved as I stood up to go. I wasn't being suspended, after all. But my body was heavy, so heavy I could hardly drag it toward the door.

"You sure you don't want to go home?" Mrs. Isaacsen said.

"No thanks," I said. I still hadn't figured out how I was going to get my torn blouse past my mother. I might have one of those miniature sewing kits in my locker . . . if I had the nerve to ever go back there again.

"You'll need to cover up that rip somehow or you'll be in violation of the dress code." Mrs. Isaacsen rolled her eyes. "We have more rules around here than they do at San Quentin." She pretended to gasp. "Did I say that?"

I couldn't help grinning at her. It might have been the first time I'd smiled all day. All week. All month?

"I have a jacket in my locker," I said. "Can you give me a pass?"

"You have a jacket in your locker?" she said. "Why? Darlin', it's hotter than a sinner at a prayer meetin' in July out there." She readjusted the sweater on her shoulders. "Of course, it's colder than a corpse in here. I wish I had a dollar for every time I asked

Maintenance to turn that air conditioner down."

"I never wear the jacket in here," I said. "It's just that when I go out in the morning, I'm always expecting it to be chilly, you know, like fall is supposed to be."

"It must be beautiful where you come from at this time of year."

All I said was, "It is." I'd stopped letting myself think about the blaze of color that was right now lining every street in Missouri , dropping its pieces into fire-colored piles I could scuffle through as I headed for my real home. Picturing myself there only made it harder to accept the palm trees that looked fake and the humid heat that wilted even your eyelashes.

"Well, come on," Mrs. Isaacsen said. "Let me walk you back to the scene of the crime and make sure you don't have flashbacks while you're there."

She opened the door for me and did that fire-crackling chuckle thing again. I wasn't convinced, though, that she was really kidding. Just then, I wouldn't have put it past myself to have some kind of melt-down when I saw my locker again. Mrs. Isaacsen must have known that, because she went into chatty-chat-chat mode as we left the counseling suite and headed for the locker area.

"I have to ask," she said. "What were you talking about when you said you didn't even take two pats of butter?"

"Oh," I said. "Back at my old school, they had these big ol' homemade rolls every day but you could only take one pat of butter. You know, the little square of butter on the paper thing?"

"How big was your school, darlin'?" she said.

"We had, like, 100 kids in each grade, seventh through twelfth."

"Well, no wonder you had homemade rolls everyday." She licked her lips, which, I noticed, had only faint traces of the lipstick she'd probably applied hours ago. "I've got to get me a job at one of those schools."

I got my jacket out of the locker without incident. Even better, I got through chemistry and math without going into uncontrolled weeping OR running into Shayla or Keesha. Even at that, I bolted from the school after the last bell like I had a hundred Shaylas on my tail and cowered in a seat on the bus midway back. I would have loved to have hidden ALL the way back, but that area was "reserved" for kids who together smelled like a cigarette factory and played Papa Roach on a boom box until the driver told them to turn it off because it wasn't allowed. I didn't want to go there. I didn't know WHERE I wanted to go just then, but I knew it wasn't there.

When I got home, I managed to get down the hall to my room with just a hello-shout to my mom, and I took off my peasant blouse and hid it in the bottom of my closet for safe-keeping until I had a chance to stitch it up. The most sneaking around I normally did was to hide Christmas presents, and the whole act of having to hide something to keep myself out of trouble broke me out in a cold sweat. I closed the closet door and leaned against it.

Decision: I would do whatever it took to put what had happened that day completely out of my mind. It was over. Why dwell on it?

That was easier said than done. I could hardly eat supper because I thought I could smell Shayla's breath in the meatloaf and it made me nauseous. I also had a hard time focusing on what anybody was saying, though as usual my six-year-old sister Bonnie did most of the talking. I knew without even hearing it that Dad said to her, about ten times, "Not another word until you take five more bites."

My parents didn't seem to notice my being even quieter than usual at the table. After all, I hadn't had a whole lot to say to them since my father had announced, back in Missouri, that he had finally found a job, after six months of unemployment, and that it meant moving to Florida. He and Mom had talked it up as if living just blocks from the bay and mere miles from the Gulf had always been my life's desire and they were finally fulfilling my dream. Never, not once, had they expressed any sympathy for what I was going through.

Not that they had time. They had their usual stuff to do, like keeping Bonnie from eating something she was allergic to, which was a full-time job in itself since she was allergic to just about everything known to the human palate, PLUS all the packing and unpacking and getting new drivers' licenses and car registrations and all the things that made my mother even more uptight than she already was.

But none of that kept my parents from remembering their expectations of me. The day Mom had checked me into Panama Beach High and I found out I couldn't register for any MAPPS classes except chemistry and had to be in regular courses instead, she said to me, "Now there's no reason at all that you can't keep your four-point-oh average."

When Dr. Vaughn had pointed out that MAPPS chemistry was very difficult and that the reason the teacher had room for me in the class was that so many kids had dropped out to avoid messing up their GPA's, Mom had just said, "Laura can do it."

Yes, Laura could do it. She could also do the dishes every night, read stories to Bonnie until she went hoarse, refrain from the slightest brush with disrespect, and act as if it were all a total joy.

Yeah, I was a little resentful. Hence, I didn't have too much to say to my parents.

So I did the dishes in silence. By hand. The dishwasher in the house they'd bought didn't work, and it was pretty far down on the list of repairs to be made. The only house my parents could afford after six months without a paycheck was a one-story fixer-upper with an unfinished garret of an attic, though my father kept saying, "But we're so lucky to have something in the Cove. This is the only place to live in Panama City."

Yeah. In the week we'd been there, my father had replaced all the faucets, redid the wiring in the kitchen so we wouldn't all be incinerated, and patched about a fourth of the roof. He spent as much time at Home Depot as he did at his job. It was easy not to show him my resentment. I never saw him.

Once I was sure my mother's critical eye wouldn't detect some spot or smudge in the kitchen that was going to destroy life as we knew it, I went to my room and did homework, which I could barely concentrate on because the very scratching of my pen across the paper reminded me of Shayla's smoking-since-birth voice.

Up-to-my-eyeballs with the whole thing, I sprawled across my bed and flipped through a teen magazine I'd talked Mom into buying at the grocery store. She'd been so preoccupied with figuring out where everything was in the Winn-Dixie—who names a store "Winn-Dixie"?—and keeping Bonnie from even smelling the peanut butter because she was, of course, allergic to it, I'm sure she didn't really know she'd given me permission to toss the magazine into the cart.

As I turned the pages, I KNEW she didn't know. I had to flip back to the cover to be sure I wasn't reading *Cosmo*, for Pete's sake. Could they get those hip-hugger jeans any LOWER?

When Bonnie flung open the door, I slapped the magazine closed and rolled over to greet her. She bounced up onto the bed, two I-Can-Read books clutched in her chubby hands. At six, she still had soft little dimples at each knuckle. I didn't want those to go away as she continued to morph out of babyness and into kid-hood. I liked to put my fingers in them when she was asleep.

She settled herself into the comforter, strawberry blonde curls bouncing. While I had been graced with my father's very thick, straight-as-a-yardstick hair, Bonnie was my mother all over. The child had ringlets—RINGLETS! She was a total cherub.

"What do?" she said. That was our usual greeting.

"I was just reading," I said. "What you do?"

"Reading too," she said. "I'm gonna read to you."

I grinned into her blue-gray eyes. "Do I have a choice?"

She looked at me blankly. "No," she said.

"Go for it," I said.

I propped up on my pillows and watched her as she sat primly in front of me, legs criss-crossed, and studied the print the size of the second row on the eye exam chart.

Here comes the tongue, I thought.

And, of course, the little pink point came out of her bow of a mouth and perched itself on her pouty lower lip. When she got older they would call that the "bee-sting" mouth. Right now I refused to call it that. The thought of anything stinging my little sister, be it bee or slap or unkind word, was about more than I could think about. Especially that night.

Man, is she going to have to face stuff like what I'm facing? I thought. *Is she going to be self-conscious about her freckles? Is she going to make friends and establish herself in a school and then be ripped out of there without so much as an "I'm sorry I'm destroying your life" from the parents? Is she going to have to fend off tobacco addicts with her backpack?*

"Laurie!"

"Huh?" I said.

"Was that good?" Even her round, ruddy-like-mine cheeks were expectant.

I gave an enthusiastic nod, though I hadn't heard a word she'd read. "Perfect," I said. "Read me the other one."

"No," she said—her favorite word next to *why,* and *kewl,* for cool. Where she'd picked that up, none of us knew.

"You read to me," she said. She picked up the magazine, plopped it into my lap, and snuggled in beside me, head warm against my arm.

It's tough to say no to that.

I opened the magazine again, carefully avoiding the ad on the first page that showed two models' hip bones, and read her some article titles as I turned the pages.

"*Body Piercing,*" I read. "*Getting pierced is no longer just for weirdos, so don't worry about decorating yourself with studs.*"

"What does that mean?" Bonnie said.

"It's talking about getting your ears pierced," I said and turned the page before she could zero in on the studs protruding from the models' lips, tongues, and navels. "Let's see—*Breaking the Rules Without Getting Busted. Tired of being a good girl? Here's how to be bad without suffering any consequences.*"

"If we're bad in my class," Bonnie said, blue eyes wide and six-year-old serious, "we get our name on the board."

"Have you gotten your name on the board yet?" I said.

"Once," she said calmly. "For talking."

"Figures," I said. I went on to read a few more titles.

Be Aggressive. Find out if you're in the driver's seat or getting run over by the opposite sex.

Get Power Over Pimples—and Get Dates.

As I turned the page, Bonnie pointed a purple-marker-stained finger at yet another model with her jeans hovering precariously over her pubic bone.

"Look, Laurie," she said. "You can see her belly button."

"Yeah, well, that's the least of her worries," I said.

I slapped the magazine closed and turned to her. "Speaking of belly buttons, look out," I said. "I think the tickle monster has just arrived!"

"No-wah!"

Bonnie squealed, but she obligingly pulled up her pajama top so I could tickle her belly until she laughed herself into hiccups. I found myself wishing I could laugh that hard. That real.

When Bonnie had gone to bed, I picked up the magazine again and studied the models. All devoid of body fat. All flashing clear-skinned, braces-less smiles or pouting into the camera like sex goddesses. All "baring it and sharing it," as one of my friends in Missouri used to say when we'd see the rare girl at the shopping center giving everybody a peek at her navel or a hint of her cleavage.

I grunted to myself. Those girls back in my hometown were Amish compared to these chicks. And the really depressing thing was, the day Mom and I had gone to the Panama City Mall, we'd seen exposed hips and thongs outlined against skin-tight jeans all over the place.

I pried my journal out from between the mattress and the box springs and uncapped a pen with my teeth. It was the only remnant of the quiet-time-with-God I used to do at night, before the Big Move was announced and God had apparently abandoned me. I used to write prayers in it, like I was talking to God. Now I mostly just whined.

I wrote:

> *Is that what I'm going to have to be like to be accepted here? That's*

so depressing! Even if Mom and Dad would LET me—like THAT's gonna happen!—I couldn't pull it off. I don't even HAVE any hips, and I'm sure not going to accomplish cleavage.

Besides, they all look trashy to me. I don't want to be like that. I want to hang out with people who wear actual clothes and are like me.

Except I don't even KNOW what I'm like anymore.

I closed the journal and my eyes. Maybe I ought to join Mrs. Isaacsen's little group.

Maybe I belonged with the other misfits.

chapterthree

When I told Mrs. Isaacsen the next day that I wanted to come to her group, her exclamation point eyebrows went up and she said, "I think this is something you'll get a lot out of. Good choice, Laura."

From then until the next Tuesday, while I continued to try to look as if I didn't care that I didn't fit in (mostly by burrowing myself like a mole into my studies), I spent the nothing-to-do hours wondering what to expect from the Group. I came up with several possible scenarios.

It could it be like, "Hello, my name is Laura and I'm a loser," and everybody would say in unison, "Hello, Laura." I saw something like that on a TV show once, only it was for alcoholics.

There could be girls there who, like me, had gotten off on the wrong foot at 'Nama High, as they called it. Maybe I would be sitting next to one of those multi-pierced girls who sold drugs, and across from a chick who was about to give birth to her second child.

Maybe Mrs. Isaacsen would make each of us tell our life story.

Or we could just sit there until somebody felt moved to say something. I'd seen that on TV, too. I hoped Mrs. Isaacsen wasn't thinking I would be the one to break the silence. The one time I HAD opened my mouth at Panama Beach High, I'd ended up slammed against a locker with somebody's nicotine teeth in my face.

As it turned out, Group was nothing like any of that.

In the first place, as I sat in one of the padded chairs in Mrs. Isaacsen's office and glanced at my fellow "patients," I didn't think any of them looked or acted like they needed therapy. As we all plastered on the name tags Mrs. Isaacsen gave us (shaped like the frogs she was obviously nuts over), I checked out each girl.

Michelle, a black girl with long, straightened hair and a full, serious mouth, had to be a senior. The way she crossed her legs and didn't fidget with anything made her look mature, like she would never stick straws up her nose or shriek with her friends in the make-up aisle at Walgreen's. I couldn't imagine what she was in here for, but it definitely wasn't for violating the dress code. She could have worn her current black pants and starched white fitted blouse to work at a CPA's office. Decision: Since she was right this minute probably thinking that I was about twelve, I needed to act more adult in front of her. I crossed MY legs—and banged the chair next to me with my sandal-exposed toes. Good start.

Next to her, Joy Beth was her total opposite. She had lanky, sort-of-blonde hair that seemed to annoy her. She kept flipping it back over her sweatshirt-clad, very hefty shoulder. The shirt had a Florida State emblem on it, but I was pretty sure she didn't care WHAT it said. It was probably the top one in the drawer when she'd stuck her hand in there to find something to wear that morning. The only part of her attire she seemed really concerned about was her tennis shoes. They were brand new and looked like something the space program had developed, and she wore them like a badge that said, *I'm a jock. Is that a problem for you?* When she glanced over and caught me staring at her, she looked straight back at me with eyes that were so pale gray they were almost clear. She widened them just enough to communicate *What?* I looked away. Decision: She didn't look like her name should be Joy ANYTHING. I needed to stay away from her.

The nametag on the next girl just said, "K.J." I was glad she was studying Mrs. Isaacsen's art display, because I couldn't take my eyes off of her get-up. She had bead earrings as long as totem poles hanging from her lobes and several beaded necklaces dipping down into a flowered peasant blouse. I was sure someone had actually worn it in the '60s. Over that was a faded denim, embroidered vest which was long enough that, with the help of a wide woven belt that tied in front with leather strings, it concealed how low her hip-hugger jeans were actually cut. Now, SHE might be in for breaking the dress code, except she pulled it off so well. If I dressed like that, people would ask me—if anyone actually ever spoke to me—why I was dressed for Halloween. K.J., on the other hand, had an air about her, like she didn't appreciate the system and had a very classy way of getting around it. That made it okay that her chin-length light brown hair looked like it hadn't seen a brush all day. Of course, it helped, too, that her skin was like something out of a Noxzema commercial and her oblong brown eyes were set wide apart so she seemed young, yet fascinating. Yeah, my guess was that *whatever* was her favorite word, and she always got away with it. Decision: I shouldn't even TRY to impress her. I'd never do it.

I had to crane my neck to see the nametag on the girl next to me. When I did, she obligingly stuck out her chest for me and said, "Celeste. The last E is silent."

I did a double take. She had an accent that could only mean she'd been born and raised in Brooklyn. It stuck out in this room full of soft-drawling Southerners.

She was also the only one in the room besides Mrs. Isaacsen who was smiling, and she had a reason to. She was very blonde, very blue-eyed, and with the smattering of freckles over her nose and the big ol' glossy-lipped grin, she pretty much defined "cute." The hat—the kind men used to wear when they drove Model Ts or played golf—the red-and-white striped T-shirt, the bell bottoms, and the red tennis shoes made her look tomboyish; but somehow I got the feeling she was anything but. Tomboys didn't stick out their breasts proudly and wrinkle their noses when they smiled and look around as if to say, "All right—so, who wants to be my best friend first?"

I sighed, sadly. Unfortunately, she wasn't the kind of girl I usually ended up being friends with. She had way too much confidence. My friends tended more toward the type who talked wistfully about what it must be like to have her guts.

Decision: I would dream of being her—as long as she got good grades. That had to be part of my image, or I basically had no image.

"All right, Mrs. I.," Celeste said. "What's the deal?"

"The DEAL," Mrs. Isaacsen said, as she squeezed a chair in-between Michelle and me, "is that I've worked with each one of you on some level—"

Joy Beth, the girl with the big shoulders, grunted.

"—and I've come to the conclusion that you could all benefit from being together for an hour, two times a week."

"That's it?" K.J. said. Her jewelry rattled as she resituated herself in her chair. This was clearly a waste of her time.

"That's it," Mrs. Isaacsen said.

Joy Beth was shaking her head. "Nah," she said. "There's gotta be more to it than that."

"Would I lie to you?"

Mrs. Isaacsen raised her brows in that way I liked. I found myself shaking my head no.

Celeste tucked her legs up under her and said, "So, where do we start?"

Her voice was husky and scrappy-sounding. I bet boys liked that voice. Being a soprano, I would never achieve it. Besides, boys didn't seem to see much in me anyway. I wasn't too sure a voice change would help.

"I just happen to have a plan," Mrs. Isaacsen said. "I'd like for each of you to tell us, just briefly, what situation spurred me to invite you to this group."

"Hello!" K.J. said. "How would we know that?"

"What happened just moments before I said this group was a good idea for you?"

Mrs. Isaacsen seemed completely unaffected by K.J.'s attitude. Even subtle as it was, my parents would be packing her off to her room for the rest of her natural life.

"Oh, I know that," Celeste said. She was waving her hand and, of course, grinning.

"Go for it," Mrs. Isaacsen said.

"I'd just gotten in trouble for making out by the lockers," Celeste said, cheerily.

I wondered vaguely if she'd done it during lunch. Double whammy.

"Well, ya think?" Joy Beth said. "That was pretty stupid."

Mrs. Isaacsen put her hand up. "Ah. I knew I forgot something. There are a few guidelines we will follow in this group."

"Rules," K.J. said.

"Guidelines," Mrs. Isaacsen said. Again, she didn't even blink as she went right on. "Number one: No cross talk. All we do in here is tell our stories. No comments. No judgments. Now, you CAN ask questions if you want."

"Oh," Joy Beth said with a grunt. She looked at Celeste. "Don't you THINK it was pretty stupid to be making out in the school building?"

"With that guy, yeah," Celeste said. "He turned out to be a jerk."

"Aren't they all?" K.J. said.

By now, Michelle was rolling her eyes and picking lint off of her pants, and I was squirming. Mrs. Isaacsen's good nature could only last so long, and I really hated it when adults yelled. I'd eat plaster if necessary, just to avoid it.

But Mrs. Isaacsen merely said, "That brings me to guideline number two: No negative talk about anyone in this room, and that includes a negative connotation to a question." She let her little bird eyes pan our faces. "Now that you know the guidelines, I'm going to be diligent about your following them."

To my surprise, Joy Beth actually looked embarrassed. And even K.J. didn't push it. It occurred to me that they all probably knew Mrs. Isaacsen better than I did, and they respected her. Still, I was relieved when Celeste said in her husky chirp, "You want I should go on?"

"I don't think we need the details of the actual event," Mrs. Isaacsen said. "Just whether you think that's what precipitated my invitation."

"All right. I got suspended on account of the lip lock and I was in here cryin' my eyes out, hopin' you'd get me out of it—"

"Not a chance."

"And then it was like you had this bright idea, and you asked me to join this group. So, I did." She looked around at us—*jauntily* I think is the word to describe it—and added, "How come there aren't any boys in here?"

Mrs. Isaacsen said dryly, "Anybody want to go next?"

Michelle raised her hand, just bent at the elbow. "I will," she said.

Her voice startled me. I'd been expecting it to be all low and sultry like Halle Berry or somebody. But she talked kind of sharp, like mothers do when their kids are getting on their nerves. So much for my expectations.

"I wanted to go on work study," she said, "you know, come here half day and have a job half day—and Dr. Vaughn wouldn't approve it, so I came to see Mrs. Isaacsen."

"Question," K.J. said.

Mrs. Isaacsen nodded at her.

"Why wouldn't Vaughn approve work study? You look like you could go straight out to work right now."

My thoughts exactly.

"Because that program is only for juniors and seniors, and I'm a sophomore," Michelle said.

"No stinkin' way!" Celeste said, and then clapped her hand over her mouth.

"I make some exceptions for spontaneous eruptions," Mrs. Isaacsen said.

"I bet you were like, so mad when you came in here, huh?" K.J. said.

Michelle shook her head, barely moving her long hair. "No point in getting mad. I just thought it was unfair." She looked at Mrs. Isaacsen and smiled politely. "At least you listened to me. So here I am."

"That's what we're about here," Mrs. Isaacsen said. "Listening."

"I don't get it," Joy Beth said. "This is a question: We're just supposed to listen to each other? How's that gonna help somebody?"

"Do I need help?" K.J. said.

As far as I could see, they were already mastering getting around the no-comment rule by turning everything into a question. I felt like I was on *Jeopardy*.

"Why don't you tell us your story?" Mrs. Isaacsen said to K.J.

I could almost picture a *Whatever* poised on K.J.'s fashionably full lips, but she went on without inserting it.

"I told a teacher off."

There was a unanimous stirring in the room. I couldn't tell if it was out of shock or admiration.

"Mr. Dennison told me I had an attitude," K.J. said with a shrug. "And I told him he was just discriminating against me because I'm the only freshman in his geometry class."

"You're just a freshman?" Celeste said.

K.J. looked at her, open-faced. "Do you have a problem with that?"

"Careful, ladies," Mrs. Isaacsen said.

"It was a fair question!" K.J. said.

The eyebrows went up. "Go on with your story."

K.J. shrugged again. "That's basically it. I mean, I told him I had a right to have any attitude I wanted as long as I did my work, and I do. I have a 98 average in that class."

"What else did you say to him?" Mrs. Isaacsen said.

"That he was the one with the attitude."

"And?"

"And that he was a gravy-sucking pig."

Michelle gasped. Celeste muffled laughter with her hand. I even said, "Are you serious?"

"What's the deal?" K.J. said. "It's from Shakespeare."

"And it should have stayed there," Mrs. Isaacsen said in her dry way.

"Yeah, that's what you told me that day," K.J. said. "And then you invited me to this group; and since I got kicked out of the play for getting suspended, I didn't have anything to do during activity period anyway."

She looked at us all with her face wide open, as if to say, "You want a piece of me?"

I did not. I shrunk back in my chair.

"What?" she said. She was looking straight at me.

"Excuse me?" I said.

"Why are you giving me that look?"

"Enough K.J.," Mrs. Isaacsen said.

It was the first sign of sharpness she'd shown; and I was so grateful for it, I had to hold myself back from kissing her loafers.

"Sorry," K.J. said, not too convincingly and to Mrs. Isaacsen, not to me.

What is it with me? I thought. *Do I have a sign on my forehead that says, "Pick on me, I've got nothing else to do"?*

"Joy Beth," Mrs. Isaacsen was saying. "Let's hear your tale."

Joy Beth slid down in the chair at a slant and crossed her arms over her chest. Even through the sweatshirt I could see that her arms were solid, like a pair of frozen hams. I'd known farm boys in Missouri who pitched hay every morning before school but they didn't have biceps that large.

"I didn't get in trouble or nothin'," she said. "I was just ticked off."

"Why?" Celeste said. She reminded me of Bonnie, the way she tilted her head at Joy Beth.

"I just was."

Mrs. Isaacsen raised an eyebrow. That, I thought, was probably going to be it.

"And what did we talk about?" Mrs. Isaacsen said to her.

"I know," Joy Beth said.

"So take your time, but tell the story."

Joy Beth crossed and re-crossed her arms a couple of times, and then she stared at the toes of her state-of-the-art shoes and said, "My parents took me off the swim team and I got mad so I came in to vent to Mrs. I."

"Why'd they take you off the team?" K.J. said.

"Because they're stupid," Joy Beth said.

I glanced at Mrs. Isaacsen, but she seemed willing to let that go. She nodded, and then she looked at me. I was still cowering in the chair.

"That just leaves you, Laura," she said.

She looked at me with a kind of softness in her eyes that was different from the way she looked at the other girls. I think that was the only reason I sat up straighter in the chair and spilled my guts about my confrontation with Shayla.

When I was finished, Celeste was staring at me, open-mouthed. "NO stinkin' way!" she said. "You actually hit Shayla Cunningham over the head?"

She sounded impressed, which made me shrink back in the chair again. "I shouldn't have," I said. "I don't believe in violence."

"Why not?" K.J. said. It was as if I had just said I didn't believe in free speech.

"It's against my religion," I said. "I'm a Christian."

For the second time that period, I was grateful for Mrs. Isaacsen's guidelines. If it hadn't been for her warning look at K.J., I'm sure I would have been thrown to the lions.

And just then, I wasn't sure I could hold my own. I hadn't talked to God in weeks.

"Our time's up for today, ladies," Mrs. Isaacsen said. "How you doin'? Do you all feel pretty comfortable for a first time?"

"I guess," K.J. said. "At least you didn't try to reform us."

"Would I have a chance?" Mrs. Isaacsen said. Her eyes were sparkling.

"No way," K.J. said.

Joy Beth was the first one to charge for the door, and Michelle and K.J. both rushed out like they had important board meetings. In Michelle's case, she might have. I started to follow them when Celeste touched my arm. I jumped like a rabbit.

"You okay?" she said.

"Yeah. I just—never mind."

She grinned. "I'd be freaked out too if Shayla Cunningham had jumped me. That chick is scary."

"Tell me about it," I said.

"You want to have lunch?"

I stopped in the midst of hauling my backpack up onto my shoulder and stared at her.

"Me?" I said.

"Yeah. Did you bring your lunch or do you buy?"

"Bring—I brought it."

"Me too. I never touch that stuff they serve here. You might as well eat the Styrofoam things it comes in. Probably taste better. Bye, Miz I."

Mrs. Isaacsen smiled at us from behind the Tupperware container she was already eating out of at her desk. I smiled back as we left, but I was a little nervous.

Okay, my stomach was turning over, my mouth was going dry, and I couldn't think of an intelligent thing to say. I hadn't talked girl talk in so long, I felt like I spoke a different language. I could already envision myself sitting at her table like I was on MUTE and nobody could find the remote.

But I shouldn't have worried because Celeste, it appeared, could carry on a conversation with a gas pump, which was about the way I was feeling anyway.

"That was like way different than I thought it was gonna be," she said. "I thought we'd have to tell some deep dark secret or somethin', which there is no stinkin' way I'm gonna do. Not with K.J. in there. Somebody needs to work that chick over. We are talkin' ATTITUDE."

Then she flashed a brilliant smile, which convinced me that she would never be the one to work anybody over.

No, Celeste was a lover, not a fighter. THAT was obvious the minute we sat down at one of the concrete tables in the courtyard.

She was still chatty-chat-chatting away about how cool Mrs. Isaacsen was, even if she DIDN'T get Celeste out of her suspension, when a boy who stood about six-foot-twenty paused in his lope across the courtyard to squeeze the back of her neck.

"Hey, baby. What's happenin'?" he said. Yikes, he had a voice like Brad Pitt, all throaty and wonderful. I concentrated on my p.b. and pickle so I wouldn't stare at him.

"Just sittin' here with Laura. You know Laura?"

I looked up just long enough to exchange nods. I never knew what to say beyond *hi*.

Didn't need to. He turned immediately back to Celeste, squeezed her neck again, and took off, tossing his parting shot over his shoulder: "Call me, now."

She wrinkled her nose at him and grinned at me. "That's Taylor

Bradshaw. He's on the basketball team."

"Ya think?" I said.

"I used to date him," she said. "He's an awful boyfriend."

I didn't have a chance to ask what constituted "awful" in a boyfriend—never having had one myself—because another guy with dark hair hanging in his face and puppy-like brown eyes was suddenly straddling her bench and gazing at her.

"What's up, dude?" she said. She had yet to take a bite of her lunch.

"I don't know," he said. "You want to come over?"

"When?"

"Tonight."

"She dumped you, didn't she?"

He attempted to look innocent, stood up, and then sat back down. The kid was making me dizzy.

"It's not just that. I want to see you."

"Give it a week," Celeste said. "Then you can see me."

"Man!"

She touched the end of his nose lightly with her finger and he was gone. It was like something out of old re-runs of *Bewitched*.

"All right," she said to me. "Tell me about Laura."

I was in mid-bite of my sandwich, and by the time I swallowed it all, two MORE boys had come by. Number 1 was in a pair of those pants two people could fit into and acted like he wanted Celeste to be one of them. He was there long enough for her to push him out of her face, all the while laughing into it. Number 2 was a Black kid who tossed her a Frisbee, which she sat on and wouldn't give back to him until he said the password Celeste insisted on: "Celeste, you rock!"

It was pretty much that way all through lunch, though I have to say she introduced me to every one of the guys that made pit stops at our table and inserted comments to me in between, like, "So I've seen you eating alone and I've wanted to introduce myself, so this is cool," and "Are you actually eating a peanut butter and pickle sandwich? Wow. Interesting."

By the time the bell rang for fifth period, I was sure I'd met half the male population of 'Nama Beach, as it was more popularly known. None of them hung around for long, but all of them seemed to think Celeste was at least some variation of a babe. That was why I felt myself spiraling down as I said good-bye to her and headed for study hall.

She was the first person who had been at all nice to me and had tried to make me feel included. But there was no way I was going to end up being friends with her. We probably didn't have anything in common—I was definitely not a boy magnet. I had never in my life been as physically close to a boy as she had been about eight times in the past half hour. That is, if you didn't count Douglas Kunkle and the insane moment freshman year when I'd let him kiss me at a choir cookout. It was a fact no one at my school in Missouri ever forgot, and it was the one and only reason I had to be glad to be away from there. But right now, I'd have given a couple tenths of a point off my GPA to be back there hearing some-body say, "You so did not kiss Douglas Kunkle—did you?"

It wasn't that my life had been exactly peaceful in Missouri. You can't be involved in as much stuff as I was and not be stressed out all the time, especially when you're trying to live up to your parents expectations of straight A's, no excuses. And especially when you know that getting into a good college is the only guaran-tee to some kind of decent future. Choir had taken a huge chunk of my time, but it was one thing I didn't mind stressing about. When I was singing, I always felt like somebody besides workaholic Laura Duffy. I know it sounds weird, but singing kind of transported me. It's what led me to be a Christian—I sang praise songs and hymns until I realized I believed them.

I hadn't sung a note since we'd moved.

I had to admit, even as I brought myself back to Panama City, Florida, and dropped into a desk in study hall, that being involved at church and at school kept me from gnawing on the fact that even the not-that-pretty girls at Harry Truman seemed to have a boyfriend. But at least I had fit in SOMEHOW, and my friends understood my drive to be perfect and my tendency to exaggerate my failures when I didn't quite reach the perfection mark, which was often.

They'd be getting an earful of it right now, I thought. I looked at the doorway where two punky guys with cans of chew placed conspicu-ously in their shirt pockets were stalling, putting off coming into the room. I actually couldn't blame them for not wanting to be here. To call this a "study" hall you had to be kidding. I was the only one who ever even opened a book, but that didn't mean I could actually concentrate. Projectiles of all descriptions were thrown across the room. Pagers went off, even at the risk of being confiscated by the teacher who basically ignored us and drowsily graded papers as if she were as bored as we were. A couple of the girls actually gave themselves complete manicures and pedicures in the back.

Yeah, being in there was like having the word *Loser* branded on your cheek. The only reason I WAS in there was because the elective I wanted, music theory, was too far along for me to catch up, so they said. I could pick it up next semester, and in the meantime, there I was with all the kids who had been kicked out of classes and sure weren't going to be studying, because if they EVER studied, they wouldn't have been kicked out of their classes and ended up in here in the first place.

Still, I had to try. Dr. Vaughn hadn't been kidding when she'd said MAPPS chemistry was difficult. I was so lost in there I about had a panic attack every time I opened my textbook.

Even as I was slowly pulling back the front cover and waiting for the cold sweat, Ms. Carter droned out, "Laura Duffy?"

She squinted around the room as if she were convinced there was no such person in her classroom.

"Here," I said.

She held up a pink piece of paper. "Note from the office for you."

"Busted," said one of the skinny guys.

"You're busted? No way," said Skinny Guy #2.

"Hey, pick us up a burger or somethin' while you're out, would ya?" said Skinny Guy #1.

"Order of fries too." Then they both laughed at each other.

"Okay," I said lamely and then scurried out of there.

Once I was safely out of study-hall-scrutiny, I let myself panic. Palms sweating around the pink message slip I was clutching, I envisioned myself prostrate before Mr. Stennis, pleading for mercy, begging him not to throw me into a closed room with Shayla and Keesha.

A door opened just a few feet in front of me, snapping me out of one horrifying vision and into another. Shayla stepped out of the door and right into my path.

chapter four

I froze. She didn't.

"Do you just go around lookin' to get your tail kicked?"Shayla said. I shook my head.

She took a menacing step toward me. I didn't smell the tobacco this time because I couldn't breathe. It was going to happen all over again, and this time there wasn't a thing I could do about it. There was no anger surging up and willing me to fling my belongings at her. There was only the kind of fear that kept me riveted to the floor.

"So . . . what?" Shayla said. "You only talk when you're bustin' somebody?"

Pretty much, I thought. *Please, just stop asking me questions and get this over with!*

"I can't believe a retard like you got me suspended," she said. And then she made that hissing sound that shot panic up through the top of my head. If the door hadn't opened again, I would have screamed.

A tall, too-thin man with a scruffy goatee emerged from what I now realized was Mr. Stennis's office, with Mr. Stennis right behind him.

"Out of the building," he said.

The scruffy man nodded and folded his fingers around Shayla's arm in a way that would have led ME directly to a straight jacket. She didn't appear to notice because she still hadn't taken her eyes off of me. They were broadcasting a message I couldn't miss: *Watch yourself, New Girl, because I WILL get you.*

Scruffy Man, whose taut look told me he had to be Shayla's father, routed her around me and disappeared around the corner. Mr. Stennis was still in the doorway looking at me.

"You okay, Laura?" he said.

"Yeah," I lied.

There was so much anxiety racing through my veins, I felt like I was being electrocuted. It was obvious now why I was there. We were all going to be suspended, all three of us; and any minute now my father was going to appear and escort ME out of the building, at which point my entire life would be over. Sure, I was okay.

I held out the now very-damp note to him. "I think I'm supposed to come see you," I said.

He took a glance at it and shook his head. "Pink's counseling," he said. "Yellow is discipline." His blue eyes crinkled as he smiled at me. "You get a yella one and you know you're in trouble. You don't want that."

NO, I don't! I wanted to shout at him. *But it's following me around!*

Mr. Stennis was looking at me curiously, probably because I hadn't moved even a fraction of an inch from the spot where Shayla had planted me. At this point, I was about to take root.

"You're a good girl, Laura," he said. "Try to stay away from the Shaylas."

Before I could assure him that that had become my life's sole purpose, he disappeared inside his office, and once again all doors were closed to me. The long hallway suddenly elongated further and I felt myself falling forward. I groped for the wall and leaned there until it stopped undulating like a fun house mirror and all the doors stopped spinning in my head. Then I knew I had to get to Mrs. Isaacsen.

I had every intention of telling her not only what had just gone down with Shayla, but also the dizzying thing that had nearly dropped me into a faint as well. But something happened as I was focusing myself down the hall. It was as if a valve shut off in me somewhere, and the panic was no longer allowed to come in. I felt flat and numb, and all I wanted to do was stay that way. At least now I was in control.

It didn't last that long.

I was fine at first. Mrs. Isaacsen let her half-glasses swing down to her chest on their chain when I came in, and with her usual brown-eyed smile got me situated in one of those chairs that were beginning to feel so comfortable to me. She sat across from me and got right to the point.

"Did you feel comfortable in Group this morning?" she said.

"Sure," I said.

The pointy eyebrows shot up.

"Well, most of the time," I said.

"I like that answer better." Mrs. Isaacsen leaned toward me. She was wearing a frog pin on her collar. "I'm always going to be completely honest with you," she said. "I want you to do the same."

"I am," I said.

"Just know that there's a difference between saying what you think you should be saying and what is really true. Whatever is said in here stays in here."

I felt a hopeful trickle of relief. "Does that mean you won't call my parents and tell them what happened with Shayla?"

She looked surprised. "You haven't told them?"

"No stinkin' way!"

Mrs. Isaacsen burst into the fire-crackling laugh. "Are you spending time with Celeste?"

"I just had lunch with her is all."

"That's all it takes!" Mrs. Isaacsen leaned back, shaking her head. "I have no intention of calling your parents, Laura. That incident is over. The books are closed. You don't need to worry about consequences because there aren't any. Done. Over. Finished."

I had to laugh. She sounded like she was ready to go for the thesaurus if I didn't get it soon.

"Okay, over," I said. I was sure it wasn't over in Shayla's mind, but I didn't go there. I gave Mrs. Isaacsen a smile.

"Now," she said, "can we move on to why I asked you to come in?"

I nodded slowly. I was already flipping through all the other reasons she could have for wanting to counsel me and none of them seemed that bad. Nothing I couldn't handle.

She eased into the back of her chair. "I wish I'd made some tea," she said. "Do you like tea?"

"The only time I ever drink it is when I'm sick," I said.

"Now that's tragic," she said. "I'm going to have to educate you. Anyway—this morning in Group, you mentioned that you're a Christian."

My heart went into spastic mode again. That was one possibility I hadn't considered.

"I'm sorry," I said. "It just came out—I mean, because it's true. I forgot I'm not supposed to talk about it in school. We didn't have to be that careful at my old school—"

Mrs. Isaacsen put her hand up, a charm bracelet jiggling from her wrist. "Now before you go throwing yourself on the mercy of the court," she said, "I have no problem with you expressing your faith in our group. In fact, I'm glad you did."

"Oh," I said. All the fears that were flinging themselves into my brain collided with each other and fell into a confused heap.

"I'm a follower of Christ too," she said. "It's my life." She put out her hand again, this time to squeeze mine. "It's always a blessing to meet someone who shares my passion."

Passion? I'd never exactly thought about my being a Christian as a passion. Wasn't that something they did in R-rated movies?

Mrs. Isaacsen's tiny eye-wrinkles had smoothed out, as if she were peaceful and pleased. I suddenly felt like a fraud. I'd promised to be honest with her, and not to be meant I couldn't remain in the room with her. Her open face commanded it.

"It's not exactly that way," I said.

"How is it?" she said. There was nothing challenging in her voice. It was just a question.

"I pray to God in the name of Christ," I said. "Well, I mean, I used to. I prayed so hard that he wouldn't make us move, and when he did it anyway, I had trouble praying after that. I know I should, but—it's hard."

"Of course it is. About nine-tenths of being in a relationship with Christ is hard."

I stared for a millisecond before I went on. "My family goes to church. Well, we did in Missouri. We haven't started here, but we haven't been here that long and my mom's trying to make the house all perfect and my dad's always working and when he isn't at work he's working on our house. Since Sunday's his day off, he does stuff on the house all day. This past Sunday, he started up some kind of power saw thing at six o'clock in the morning."

"The man should be shot," Mrs. Isaacsen said mildly.

"I was into church back in Missouri," I said. "Probably more than my parents. I was secretary of my church youth group."

"Of course you were."

"Is that the same as being passionate?"

"It's an important piece of it, I'm sure. How does your family feel about God?"

That one really caught me off guard.

"Feel?" I said. "I don't know how we feel. We don't talk about God around the house. We say grace before meals and I say prayers with Bonnie—she's my little sister—when she goes to bed. But it's not like we discuss it at the dinner table or anything. I know my parents believe in God or we wouldn't go to church. They're not like some of my friends' parents, though—back home—in Missouri. They were like, 'Praise the Lord' when something good happened, or they'd say, 'I'll pray for you' when something bad went down. Even some of the girls in my youth group, they talked about their walk with the Lord all the time. I kind of wanted that, but I know my parents would totally not, I don't know—"

"Take a breath, Laura," Mrs. Isaacsen said.

"Oh, sorry," I said. "I always go all chatty when I'm not sure what to say." A giggle slipped out. "I guess I just say everything!"

"Everything you can say before you pass out," Mrs. Isaacsen said. Her voice was dry, but her eyes were soft. "There is no need to worry about what to say in here. Sounds like you're being very honest." She resituated in the chair. "We are definitely going to have tea next time."

"There's going to be a next time?" I said.

"If you want. Would you like to come in every now and then and we'll talk about our faith journeys?"

I looked down at my hands, which were frantically trying to dry themselves on the thighs of my Tommy Jeans. "I don't think I have a journey right now," I said. "I think my faith-car broke down or something."

She chuckled. "Then would you like some help getting it started? You said you wanted what those girls back in Missouri had with our Lord."

"Is that legal?" I said. "I mean, won't you get in trouble for talking about God stuff in here?"

"What the two of us talk about is purely between us," she said, "unless you feel coerced in some way. "

"No!" I said. "I want to—only—"

"Only—?"

I shrugged miserably. "I don't know. I mean, I don't see what good it will do. You told me to be honest, and, I just don't think it's going to change anything. I'm still going to have to live here and not have friends or the life I used to have and I can't get the classes I need so I probably won't get into a good college now and all I have going for me is to get an education because nobody's sure ever going to marry me since I'm sixteen and I've never even had a boyfriend and I just have to DO something with my life and how's God going to change that when my parents obviously aren't listening to him—"

Whatever else there was to say, I couldn't say it because I was crying too hard.

"I don't even know why I'm crying," I said.

"It's okay, darlin'. I bought more Kleenex." She handed me a wad. "You blow and I'll talk."

I nodded and honked away.

"Now, before we go any further," she said, "I need to be very clear on what I'm about. I make no apologies for being passionate about God. And I make no bones about why I'm helping you. This is about you being transformed into Christ's likeness. Period." It was her turn to take a breath. "Are you good with that?"

By now I'd pretty much filled three tissues and could once again be coherent. It was hard not to be when somebody was being that in-your-face. My Midwestern upbringing was suddenly shaken up and opened like a bottle of pop. But it was the first thing that had sounded clear and definite to me in a long time.

"Okay," I said. "I don't know if I'm ever going to be THAT good, but I can try."

Mrs. Isaacsen shook her head. Even as I watched her, her eyes were changing from their merry twinkle to what I was figuring out was passion. I wasn't sure I'd ever seen it before, on anybody. "Trying is the least of it, Laura," she said. "This is something you have to ALLOW to happen."

Uh-oh. Not something I did too well.

It was as if she could see that. She settled back in the chair and took on a more matter-of-fact air. "You understand the powers of the world, don't you?" she said.

I considered that. "I understand the powers the world has OVER me right now," I said.

"Who has that power?"

"My parents. The school."

"Go deeper."

I grunted. "Shayla. The popular kids who decide what's cool for everybody."

"Do you have any of that power?"

I didn't even have to think about that one. "No. Right now, I don't have control over anything. Not one thing!"

I clutched at the arms of the padded chair, digging my fingernails in. The same anger I'd felt the day I'd clobbered Shayla was rising up in me—only this time there was nobody I could attack.

Mrs. Isaacsen got back in my face. "If you want power, Laura," she said, "you need to understand the secret powers of God—the powers you can have through your connection with him."

"But I don't trust him!" I said. "I'm mad at him!"

"But at least you still believe in him. You can't be angry at someone you don't even think is there—and right now, you're angry."

"But there's nothing I can do about it! All it does is make me want to—"

"—Hit people over the head with your backpack?"

"Yes!"

By now, Mrs. Isaacsen's nose was almost touching mine, and her eyes were on fire.

"Then trust God beyond your circumstances—trust Him beyond your own strength."

"If I do that, will he send me back to Missouri?"

She shook her head, never taking her fiery eyes from mine. "God doesn't take away the problem. He gives you a different solution, and that solution lies in the powers only he can give you."

"Then he better give me some of those," I said. "Because I don't know what else to do."

"That is the perfect place for you to be," Mrs. Isaacsen said. She still wasn't letting go of my eyes. "God is an incredible opportunist. He'll use wherever you are, whatever problem you're facing, to give you power."

My eyes were now burning right back at hers, I could feel them. "Tell me how to get them."

"You can't 'get' them—you have to open yourself up and accept them."

"That doesn't help me! What do I DO?!"

"Look at the problem. Don't pray that it will be removed. Pray for new answers. Then receive the healing."

My teeth tightened. "I can't pray."

"Then first you have to surrender."

"Surrender! That's all I do, so everybody can push me around and move me like I'm a checker on a board—"

"Not to people. To God. You want to follow Christ like your friends?"

I couldn't answer.

"If you do, the first step is to say, 'All right, my Lord, take over. I'm giving my life to God and I want you to show me how. I'm trusting you completely to show me the Way.' Then you commit yourself to love and trust in Christ, believe he came directly from the Father, believe the Father loves you directly."

"Okay," I said through my teeth, "I commit—"

"No, no." Mrs. Isaacsen put her finger almost to my lips. For the first time, she drew back from me, and I realized we had been nose-to-nose for a long time, and that I'd practically been shouting into her face. I put my own hand over my mouth and was terrified.

"It's all right," she said. "You did exactly what you needed to do. You were honest. God wants that. Now keep being honest. Jesus will rise and come to life in you, and you will have a knowing that can't be explained. Then you will have power. Let it be real. Pray and listen, and it will come to you."

I reached for the Kleenex again. "I used to feel that," I said. "When I was singing."

"Did you stop singing?"

"Yeah. I didn't feel like there was anything to sing about."

"I hear you," she said. "It's easy to praise him when everything is going our way. The challenge is to live beyond what we can see and touch. That's the way Jesus lived. We can't miss God that way." Once again, her eyes took on their passion-glow. "That's where the power is."

I nodded, although I wasn't sure what I was agreeing to. At the moment, I felt a little like something out of *Harry Potter*. I had just felt and said things that had to have come out of somebody else. I was somebody else when I was in this room—and I wasn't sure I wanted to be her at all.

"Yes? No?" Mrs. Isaacsen said, tilting her head from side to side.

"I don't know."

"That's better than a no. Pray about it, as best you can. I'll pray. Then let's talk next week and see what God does. Fair enough?"

"Yes," I said.

The bell rang as I left her office, and I was once again Laura

Duffy engulfed in a crowd of students hurrying to things they had to look forward to and feeling as if I had nothing. That somebody else was left in Mrs. Isaacsen's chair.

All but the linty little piece I couldn't shake.

The week before Mrs. Isaacsen and I talked again passed surprisingly quickly, considering how the first week I'd been at 'Nama High had dragged like it was wearing cement shoes.

First of all, every day at lunchtime, Celeste found me and invited me to eat with her. Aside from the huge relief of having somebody to talk to, it would have been worth it just to check out the ensemble of the day.

One day she looked like she'd just retro-jetted out of the Seventies, with red-and-white checked hip huggers that had bell bottoms big enough to shelter a family of rabbits for the night.

Another day she was all romantic, with lace sleeves and pearl earrings dangling down and pale pink lipstick. And then the very next day, she showed up in this collage of colors and prints that made her look like something out of Japanese animation. Then there was the Bohemian look with all this leather fringe and blue jeans that appeared to have been run over by a truck. Basically, she was a different person everyday.

But it didn't seem to matter to the boys WHAT persona she took on. It wouldn't have made any difference to them if she'd shown up dressed like Eminem. They would probably still have passed through there drooling over her and teasing her and leading her on and letting her lead them. It was like a game and I could never figure out the rules.

Unfortunately, I did try to play it one day. I was afraid Celeste was going to dump me as a lunch partner if I didn't start doing more than just saying a lame, "Hi," every time she introduced me to a new male. So when a guy named Adam stopped by, I picked him to try to be friendly to. He wasn't as drop-dead cool as a lot of the guys—which meant he actually noticed I existed—and he'd been there several times before so it would have been weird for me not to say SOMETHING. When Celeste got up to go throw something away—which I had figured out was part of the game so they could watch how cute she looked from the back—I took a deep breath and said, "So, hi."

Adam smiled at me, rather curiously, seeing how I'd already said "Hi," when he'd arrived.

"Um, aren't you in my history class?" I said. I knew he wasn't, but it was the only thing I could think of to say.

"I don't take history," he said.

"Oh," I said. I hadn't prepared myself for any follow-up, so I spat out the next thing that came to me. "Well, it must be somebody who looks like you."

He leaned across the table, still smiling. "Baby," he said, "nobody looks like me."

"Oh, yeah, huh?" I said. And then I figured it was MY turn to go throw something away before I started blubbering out the alphabet or something. I grabbed my tray and took off for the trashcans.

"Hey!" he said.

I didn't stop or look back because Celeste never did when they called to her. Besides, what would I have said if I had? I dodged around several trash-laden people and dumped my tray unceremoniously into a garbage can.

Except that as I watched its contents fall into nasty oblivion, I realized it wasn't my tray. It was Adam's.

After that, I left the flirting to Celeste and just watched her work. If it bothered her that I didn't chat with her string of guys, she never said so.

I was starting to get into my classes too. My mother had been right, it was easy to make A's in the regular courses because I had been in honors and advanced placement classes back home. Just to make sure, though, I did a lot of extra credit and raised my hand every time the teacher asked a question. My English teacher Mrs. Wrenn wrote stuff on my papers like, "It is a joy to have you in class." Things like that could warm me for, oh, about fifteen seconds.

Dr. Vaughn had also been right—about MAPPS chemistry. The teacher, Mr. Frohm, who was the baldest man I had ever seen, explained everything about ten times, but most of it ended up in a jumble of elements and compounds and unsolvable equations in my brain. I took little comfort in the fact that I obviously wasn't the only one who was completely lost.

All the pretty girls with even teeth and flawless make-up and wardrobes sat together and said, "Huh?" a lot.

The jocks, boys and girls, clustered in the front and wailed, "If I'm not passing by Friday, I don't play." One black kid, obviously a basketball player because when he stretched he took up half the classroom, spent almost every class with his face in his hands like he was headed for sure doom.

I somehow ended up with the kids who were getting some of it, and who were so busy trying to get more they had hardly noticed that I had appeared on the scene. The girl on one side of me, who wore glasses and had really wild red hair, did look at me now and then and to say, "Do you EVEN know what he's talking about?" I usually shook my head and kept taking notes.

One thing Mrs. Isaacsen had said to me—about asking for different answers to the problem—struck me one day in class, and while everybody was struggling over a set of problems Mr. Frohm had given us for homework, I went up to his desk and said, "Um, are there any tutors or anything?"

He looked up at me, and I almost had to squint from the glare of the lights on his shiny forehead.

"Tutors?" he said.

I immediately felt stupid, but my perfect four-point-oh average hung over me like a silver sword.

"Yes," I said. "I really need some help in here."

"You think so?" he said. There was no trace of sarcasm in his voice. He was, in fact, looking at me like he'd never seen me before.

"Laura Duffy," I said helpfully.

"Yes, I know." He took off his glasses and peered at me. He had very black, hawk-like eyes. "Do you really think you're doing that poorly?"

"I'm not getting an A," I said.

"I see." He nodded slowly. "I'll see what I can do," he said. "Now, it may have to be after school."

"I can do that," I said.

What ELSE did I have to do?

My mother actually answered that question for me that very afternoon. When I got off the bus, she and Bonnie were out in the front yard having a tea party on a blanket and I was invited to join them.

"We're celebrating," Bonnie said.

I took the miniscule cup of "tea" she handed me. It looked suspiciously like the unfiltered apple juice she was allowed to drink. It was some of the nastiest stuff on the planet.

"Celebrating what?" I asked, as I pretended to drink under Bonnie's vigilant gaze.

"Mommy got a job!" she said.

I turned to stare at my mother. She was perched primly at the edge of the blanket, her older-cherub face looking slightly pleased with itself. I noticed for the first time that her usually combed-with-a-rake pony tail 'do had been exchanged for a cute, Katie Couric style, and she was actually wearing make-up and panty-hose and the skirt to the only suit she owned, which she normally saved for funerals.

"Did somebody die?" I said.

Mom gave me her Laura-what-ARE-you-talking-about look. "No," she said. "I went to a job interview and they hired me on the spot."

"A job?" I said. "Why?"

She selected a homemade granola bar from a doll-sized plate and offered me one. I shook my head. Granola and braces don't mix.

"Your father and I had to take out some loans when he was out of work," she said, almost under her breath, as if it weren't something you discussed in polite company. "This new job pays well, but if we're going to get out of debt any time soon, I have to help out."

"But how are you going to work?" I said. I looked significantly at Bonnie.

"I'm going to need your help," she said.

Bonnie leaned across Mom's lap to get closer to my ear, as if anybody on the block could actually hear her.

"You're gonna take care of me after school!" she said. "We get to play every day!"

I looked blankly at my mother.

"I'm going to need for you to pick her up from the elementary school every day," she said, "and stay with her until I get home at six. You'll just have to leave right after school and get off at an earlier bus stop and walk to the school—it's just a couple of blocks." She patted my leg with false cheerfulness. "Don't you want to know what kind of work I'll be doing?"

"Sure," I said.

But I barely heard her rattle off the fact that she would be working as a salesperson in the lingerie department at Dillard's department store, and that there was even room for advancement. If she did a good job and played her cards right, she might even become a certified bra consultant.

All I could hear was the sound of the last of my power slipping away.

chapter five

It wasn't that I resented Bonnie. At all. I'd been crazy about the kid from the day she was born.

I was nine at the time, and Mom was sick for a while after she delivered—she kept saying it was because she was just getting too old to have babies—so I got to help a lot. At nine, you don't see it as a chore. You see it as an honor not bestowed on many.

From age six weeks, Bonnie smiled every time she saw me.

By four months, she was practically turning inside out every time I walked into the room.

Mine was the first name she spoke. I didn't count Ma-Ma and Da-Da, which in my opinion were only accidental baby sounds. "Lau-ree," spoken distinctly through cherub lips, was worth every dash to the bathroom to get Mom a washcloth and every errand to the kitchen to get another bottle and every trip to the doctor's office where I was given the job of distracting my baby sister while somebody ran yet another battery of tests to find out why she threw up everything we gave her and broke out in hives at the drop of a hat and had a nose that ran like an old faucet.

It turned out she was allergic to everything. Everything except me.

So the prospect of babysitting every afternoon after school didn't raise any rancor in me against HER. But it definitely upped the ante on my anger at my parents, and there was plenty of that to begin with.

It was hard for me to forget my father's nasty, depressed moods back when he was jobless. I could never be quiet enough or supportive enough or cooperative enough to keep him from exploding. You don't just let something like that go, especially when even after he got his new job he never said he was sorry. We didn't talk about it, just like we didn't talk about anything else.

And it was hard for me to forgive my mother who either stressed like no other or covered up all her anxiety with this cheerful thing she did that drove me nuts. How could she pretend to be happy when I was miserable? Basically, she expected me to act like I was delighted, too, like it was my job along with everything else that was expected of me.

Yeah, so this new babysitting job stirred all of that up and added some more to it. It wasn't too tough to hug Bonnie when she ran into my arms at the school every day and it wasn't all that hard to listen to her go on—and on and on—about every tiny first-grade thing that had happened all day. But when I had her parked in front of *Sponge Bob* while I was in the kitchen measuring out her allergy medicines that had to be given at the specific times noted on the detailed instructions my mother had written out, which took up the whole refrigerator door, and preparing the complicated combinations of granola and apples and wheat germ that replaced Cheetos and animal crackers, I seethed. It was a word I was beginning to understand well.

I seethed so much, in fact, that I wasn't even tempted to sneak a can of Pringles while Bonnie munched on my healthy concoctions. Seething makes eating almost impossible. And my seething didn't stop when Mom came home at six and I was off Bonnie-duty. Or even when I was in my room by myself. I gritted my teeth the MOST when I was in bed trying to sleep.

By the second week, I was so tied up in a knot, one night I didn't doze off until about three in the morning, which meant I slept through my alarm and had to run to the bus with wet hair streaming out behind me. Of course we were having a chemistry quiz that afternoon, and I was so out of it, I knew before I even went to class that I was going to blow it. I went to see Mr. Frohm between first and second periods and said to him, "Have you, like, had a chance to find a tutor for me yet?"

He took his glasses off and peered at me again. I was tempted to say, "Laura. Laura Duffy," but he headed me off with a nod.

"I'm working on it," he said. "The trouble is, no one in class is doing well enough to tutor you. Low year."

That wasn't encouraging.

"But I do have one student from last year who is currently in my physics class. I'm trying to convince him to do it."

I would have offered to pay this genius, but I didn't have a dime to my name. I just said, "Thanks for trying."

Naturally, that was the day our Group met. I was pretty much liking the meetings so far. It was interesting hearing the other girls' stories—especially since THEY had lives—and getting to actually say something myself once in a while that people had to listen to. I was really careful not to get Joy Beth or K.J. hostile, so things were going pretty well.

But that day, I felt dizzy by the time I got to Mrs. Isaacsen's office. Everything seemed to be physically spinning out of control, just like the day I ran into Shayla outside Mr. Stennis's office. It was all I could do not to look like I couldn't hold a thought in place for more than ten seconds.

Celeste was the only one there besides Mrs. Isaacsen when I arrived. She patted the chair next to her as usual.

"What's up wit you?" she said. "Ya look terrible."

"How compassionate of you, Celeste," Mrs. Isaacsen said mildly.

"It's okay," I said. "I overslept this morning and I didn't get to eat breakfast."

"Sounds like the story of my life everyday," Celeste said. "Which is why I carry these." She produced a mini 3 Musketeers Bar and tucked it into my hand.

"Thanks!" I said. Suddenly I wanted to cry. I could actually feel my eyes tearing up for no apparent reason.

THAT definitely had to go before Joy Beth and K.J. came in. Having Michelle join us at that moment was bad enough. I sniffed back the tears, and Michelle handed me a Kleenex. She was the only teenage girl I knew who actually carried them, in a little plastic thing in her purse. She couldn't be a sophomore. She had to be at least thirty-five years old. I still hadn't figured out what she was doing in here. What any of us was doing in here.

Mrs. Isaacsen seemed to think it was a good time to reveal just that. When everybody was there and we'd dispensed with the usual preliminary whining about no toilet paper in the restroom and every teacher thinking his or hers was the only class you had while piling on the homework, she pulled out a small printed poster glued to cardboard, which she propped up on her desk for us to see. There were three questions on it:

WHO AM I?
WHERE DO I BELONG?
WHAT AM I WORTH?

I took one look at it and started bawling.

"What the heck?" Celeste said.

Her arm went immediately around me. Michelle handed me the entire plastic packet of Kleenex. Joy Beth folded her arms and looked at me like she was not surprised that I had lost my mind.

"What the heck, dude?" K.J. said. "How can you cry when she hasn't even said what it's about yet?"

"Tone, K.J.," Mrs. Isaacsen said.

"I just asked a question," K.J. said.

"She doesn't have to answer it."

I didn't, though I knew what I would have said. I was crying because I didn't know the answers to Mrs. Isaacsen's questions. Or maybe because I did.

WHO AM I? *I have no idea!*

WHERE DO I BELONG? *Certainly not here!*

WHAT AM I WORTH? *Nothing. Absolutely nothing. Not without my activities and my friends and my choir and my grades. Nothing.*

I dabbed at the tears on my face, choked the rest back, and handed Michelle the remains of her Kleenex. Mrs. Isaacsen was watching me.

"Thank you, Laura," she said.

"What did she do?" Joy Beth said.

"She exposed her vulnerability."

I felt as if I'd just exposed my navel. Maybe my entire fanny. I could feel my face going scarlet.

"That's a good thing?" Joy Beth said.

"Yes it is, and I'd like to see more of it —when each of you is ready to let us see more of yourself. Otherwise, your time here is wasted. I'm giving you a safe place to speak where you know I will protect you from judgment."

K.J., for once, shot up her hand instead of blurting her question right out.

"Question?" Mrs. Isaacsen said to her.

I could see K.J. trying to figure out how to turn some biting remark into a query. I held my breath. I had reason to.

"Then how come I feel like I'm being judged in here?" K.J. said finally.

"Do you?" Mrs. Isaacsen said.

"Yeah." She pointed right at me. "By her."

"How can you say Laura is judging anybody?" Celeste said. "She hardly opens her mouth, and when she does, she's, like, Polly-freakin'-anna or somethin'!"

"That's just it—isn't it?" K.J. said. "She's little Miss Perfect and she makes me feel like I'm supposed to consider myself some kind of low-life."

"We're getting into cross talk here," Mrs. Isaacsen said. "Not allowed. In the first place, K.J., nobody can MAKE you feel anything. That's your stuff. You want to tell us about it?"

K.J.'s wide-set eyes grew big and innocent and she said simply, "No."

As usual, Mrs. Isaacsen was unruffled. She turned to her list of questions. "In case anybody's worried," she said, "I'm not going to ask any of you to answer these right now. I just have them up here because I think these are the questions you're all battling with right now. Finding the true, real, authentic answers to them is a good goal for all of you."

K.J. raised her hand as if she were going to rattle off her answers right then. Mrs. Isaacsen ignored her.

"So how do we find the answers?" Michelle said.

I looked at her in surprise. We all did. I would have thought she already had hers typed out in triplicate and filed in a cabinet some place. As it was, she looked like she was ready to take notes.

"I think you have to start by having a philosophy of life, an unchanging set of values or standards that you live by. That becomes a frame of reference that enables you to answer those questions and truly live by the answers."

Celeste shot up her hand. "I know one of my rules."

"I can't wait," Mrs. Isaacsen said, eyes twinkling.

"Math geeks make good dates because they haven't had that much experience with kissing, so you can mold them."

There was a chorus of guffaws.

"You are outrageous, Celeste," Mrs. Isaacsen said.

"I have another one." Celeste was sitting straight up in the chair, cross-legged even in her cowboy boots and jeans. "Don't get into the serial relationship thing."

"What's that?" I said.

"One relationship after another," Celeste said. "Just date around and don't get attached to any one guy."

Oh, I thought. *That explains a lot.* Nobody could say Celeste wasn't living by her philosophy.

"What if you got a philosophy," Joy Beth said, "only nobody lets you live by it?"

"Like what?" asked Mrs. Isaacsen.

"No limits," Joy Beth said without hesitation. "That's the rule I live by. If I can dream it, I can do it. Period."

I stared at her in amazement, and so did everybody else, even K.J. It was probably the first positive thing any of us had heard her say. For a minute there, I liked her. I even envied her.

"And what IS your dream, Joy Beth?" Mrs. Isaacsen asked. Her voice was soft, so I figured she already knew the answer.

"To be an Olympic swimmer," Joy Beth said.

"So be an Olympic swimmer. What's the big wow?" Celeste blurted. "You sure got the body for it."

"Yeah, but didn't your parents make you quit the swim team?" K.J. said.

"Yeah," Joy Beth said. "They did." Then she crossed her arms over her sweatshirt and that was it. Even Mrs. Isaacsen didn't try to get anything else out of her. I suddenly felt kind of connected to Joy Beth.

Her parents made her give up something she loves, I thought, *I know that thing.* The tears welled up again, without an invitation from me. The bell miraculously rang, Michelle dropped the Kleenex in my lap and left, and Mrs. Isaacsen asked me if wanted to come in during study hall. I nodded yes and groped around for my back-pack. Celeste already had it on her shoulder, along with her own, which today, I realized, was a saddlebag.

"All right, no males today," she said as she half-dragged me toward the cafeteria. "We need to have some major girl talk ."

Actually, it was more like SHE talked and I listened, which was fine because I couldn't stop crying. Even though she picked a far corner of the courtyard instead of her usual center table, I was still drawing stares. Celeste ignored them. She sat with her back to the rest of the world, her face in mine, and proceeded to tell me exactly what I needed.

"You gotta get hooked up," she said.

"With what?" I said.

"A boy," she said patiently.

"Yeah, right. I'm almost seventeen years old and I've never had a boyfriend. I've never even been kissed, except once, but that doesn't count because he was a geek—and I DIDN'T want to mold him!"

Celeste grinned and toyed thoughtfully with her cowboy bolo tie. The only thing missing was a ten-gallon Stetson hat.

"What do you want in a boy?" she said.

"Who says I want one?"

"Your heart does. I can tell. I'm an expert on these things."

"But you said no serious relationships!"

"I said no SERIAL relationships. YOU want one that's going to last. You weren't meant to be single. Now come on, focus already. What do you want in a guy?"

Since it looked like she might break out a rope and lasso me if I didn't cooperate, I sighed and tried to collect my boy-thoughts. There were some. Just because I'd never had a boyfriend didn't mean I hadn't dreamed of having one—or two—or three . . .

"Okay," I said. "First of all, he's got to be a Christian."

"No joke?"

"No," I said. At least there had been guys in my Christian youth group in Missouri who were nice to me, who I was friends with. They weren't what you called cute, but they were nice. I could do nice.

"Christian," Celeste said. "Gotcha. What else?"

"Nothing else!" I said. "I don't know why we're even having this conversation. I'm not going to find a boyfriend!"

"No," Celeste said. "I'm gonna find one FOR you."

Even when the end-of-lunch bell rang and I went off to study hall, she was still musing over where she was going to find me a "Christian dude." I had to admit, it was kind of fun to think about, but I knew she wasn't going to be able to pull if off, so I let it go at fun. It was a nice feeling to know that she cared enough about me to try to "hook me up," as she put it. It was something I could hold onto.

I was still "holding" when I got my pass from study hall and showed up in the counseling suite to see Mrs. Isaacsen. The secretary told me she was in with another student and she'd be with me in a minute.

I wonder if it's somebody else from our Group? I thought.

Joy Beth? She was pretty upset today. I bet she's never gonna tell us what's really going on with her parents. I'd sure like to know, though, because she and I are kind of in the same place. With parents who are totally out to lunch.

Or, maybe it's Michelle? She seemed pretty interested in finding out the answers to those three questions. Who isn't? Well, probably K.J. isn't. She probably thinks she's got it all figured out already. Maybe that's why she scares me—

"Do you LIVE at the office?"

The gravelly voice brought me straight up out of my thoughts. There was Shayla, standing right over me.

From where I sat, looking helplessly up at her, her long face seemed distorted, as if her head were being pulled into some elongated shape. And then I realized she was pulling her lower lip in hard, so she'd look more threatening. It was working.

"You," she said. "YOU did this!"

Her finger came at me, landing like a missile in the middle of my chest. All around us, doors flew open. Mrs. Isaacsen was suddenly there, extricating me from the bench. Behind Shayla, the scruffy-chinned man grabbed her arms and pulled her back.

"You can't let her out of your sight, man, I'm telling ya!" Mr. Stennis said. He, too, had appeared from behind one of the closed doors. Beside him was another guidance counselor, a man whose I'm-here-to-help-you veneer had cracked into near-panic. I figured he had to be Shayla's counselor.

"Well, Laura," Mr. Stennis said to me. "You always seem to show up in the wrong place at the wrong time, don't you?"

"Any place with her is the wrong place and the wrong time," Shayla said.

She tried to twist around to bore her eyes into me again, but Scruffy Man had her well-restrained, for a change. Only when he spun her around to head her toward the door did I realize he had her in handcuffs. I'd never seen anybody in real handcuffs before. I started shaking, hard.

Mrs. Isaacsen pulled me away from the scene and ushered me quickly into her office. True to her word, she had a pot of hot tea ready. She poured me a cup, tucked it into my hands, and wrapped her sweater around me until my knees finally stopped knocking and my teeth stopped chattering.

"You okay, darlin'?" she said.

"No," I said. "My insides feel like Jell-O."

"I love those images you come up with," she said, grinning at me. "You want to talk your way out of that Jell-O?"

"I don't know what to say."

"I'm sure you'll think of something. Just take a deep breath and let 'er rip."

"I was just sitting there!" I said. "And then there she was, out of nowhere. It's like she always knows when I'm feeling like a cat's bare belly and then whammo, there she is, ready to attack!"

"A cat's bare belly," Mrs. Isaacsen said softly.

"And then those handcuffs freaked me out! I thought MY father was strict!"

"That wasn't her father. That was her probation officer. You're dealing with a pretty tough cookie here."

"You mean, like the police?"

"I mean, like, an officer of the court. After her attack on you, they finally had enough to take her to juvenile court, and the judge finally did something about it. One of MY rules of life is that we ought to do away with bureaucracy."

She softened again and nodded toward the cup of tea I was still clutching. "That's Earl Grey," she said. "Drink. Now, I know Shayla scares the beejeebers out of you, but is something else going on? That was a pretty strong reaction you had."

"I don't know," I said. "I guess it's the same old thing."

"Are you sick of it yet?" she said.

"I'm sick of people running my life!"

Mrs. Isaacsen put down her own cup and rubbed her hands together. Her face was suddenly glowing.

"Then Laura Duffy," she said. "I think it's time we got you some power, girl. Are you ready for it?"

It was as if I had no choice. If I said no, my relationship with her was over, and I was holding onto that like I was to every other string that I found dangling in front of me. What I was sick of was all the doors being closed. This one, at least, was open.

"Yes," I said to her. "I'm ready for some power."

"Then hang onto your Nikes, honey," she said, " because here it comes."

chapter six

I found myself clinging to the arms of the chair. I think I was half-expecting God himself to make an appearance, or at the very least an angel, glowing against the cinderblock walls of Panama Beach High, ready to transport me.

Anyway, what I did see was the life sparkling in Mrs. Isaacsen's eyes as she scooted her chair closer to mine to speak. Her words were warm, as if they themselves carried power.

"First of all," she said, "the Way of Christ is vigorous and requires your total attention. This isn't going to be a matter of just going to church, even though that's an important piece of it."

"Okay," I said. I wasn't afraid of hard work. If she would just give me the directions, I could certainly follow them. My four-point-oh was proof of that.

"There's something else, too. I want you to understand that this place where you are, this confused, lost-feeling place where you burst into tears without knowing why, this very place is where someone needs to be before she can find her power in God."

"So you're saying God put me here?" I said. That idea stung me, right at the back of my neck.

"I'm saying you're here and God can use you here. It's called a *liminal space*—and it's a spiritual position where human beings hate to be, but where God is always leading us."

"Have you been there—here?" I said.

"Oh, honey," she said, "you have no idea. Yes, I've been there, so I know whereof I speak."

"I don't get it," I said. I knew I was sounding childish and stubborn, but I was feeling way too weary to be anything else. This wasn't what I was expecting, what she'd practically promised me.

"Liminal space," she said, "is when you've left the tried and true behind and haven't quite been able to replace it with anything else."

That sounded like me, all right.

"It's when you're in-between your old comfort zone and any new possible answer. And in your case, you really can't go back to your old comfort zone, and you haven't been able to recreate it here. Which is not all together a bad thing."

"It's a horrible thing!" I said. I was once again turning into somebody else. She made it impossible not to. Real feelings just spewed right out of me when I was with her.

"Very few of us know how to stay on the threshold," she said. "We just feel stupid there."

"I have feeling stupid down to a science right now!"

"So here you are in this holy aimlessness," she said. "But there is a key to your power to overcome it."

Okay. Now we were talkin'.

I held my breath, ready for her next words to change everything, to make it all go away. I even closed my eyes as I said, "What's the key?"

"Listen," she said.

I waited. The frog clock ticked. Another door in the counseling suite squeaked opened and sighed closed. A kid hollered to another kid and was hushed by the secretary. But Mrs. Isaacsen didn't say anything. I opened my eyes and looked at her.

"I'm listening," I said. "What's the key?"

"That IS the key," she said. "You have to listen. Simply listen."

"To what?" I said. The mystery thing was starting to get to me now. I wanted answers, CONCRETE answers, darn it!

"Listen to God," she said.

My heart sank all the way down and landed with an angry thud.

"That's it?" I said.

"That's a lot," she said.

"But what if he doesn't say anything?"

"He will. If you're quiet enough, you'll hear it."

I squirmed in the chair and wished I had someplace to put this blasted teacup down. This conversation didn't feel cozy to me anymore.

"So I'm just supposed to sit there and wait until he says something?" I said. "I can't imagine myself doing that."

Mrs. Isaacsen grinned at me, eyes sparkling. "You're taking me at my word on this honesty thing, aren't you?"

"You said—"

"I did, and I'm glad you're doing it. It's refreshing. It usually takes someone weeks to be as open with me as you are."

"I'm desperate," I said.

"You're liminal."

Whatever! Why couldn't she just get to it?

"I'm not going to tell you to just listen and then shove you out the door," Mrs. Isaacsen said.

"Then you ARE going to tell me what to do," I said.

"I'm going to give you suggestions. Now, another guideline, and this is right up there with being honest." Mrs. Isaacsen moved to the edge of her chair. Her face was solemn. "Do NOT set me up as an authority over your life, especially when it comes to God. Let Jesus be your authority on God. Surrender to him, not me."

I squirmed some more. This time, it must have been visible because she said, "What?"

"Surrender," I said. "I don't like that word. Can't we use something else?"

"I guess we could," she said. "But let me put it to you this way. When you surrender completely to God, he makes you strong enough so that you never surrender to anyone else. Not to Shayla, not to a boy, not to what the world expects of you that you know isn't you."

I was still skeptical. She knew it. I was getting used to her knowing what I was thinking.

"Okay, next chance you get," she said, "read about the woman at the well. She surrendered so easily to Jesus. It was part of her femaleness—not a weakness, a strength. We have it so much easier than the men when it comes to giving it all to God."

"Yeah, I guess," I said slowly. "I can't imagine my dad 'giving it all to God.'"

"Jesus told the woman at the well that she had to engage her spirit in the pursuit of truth. That's what he's telling you too."

"You heard him?"

"I read it."

"O-oh," I said. "So I listen by reading the Bible. " Why couldn't she just have said that in the first place?

"That's one way," she said. "I'm going to give you some little suggested snippets to read, but only snippets. And I don't want you to STUDY them. I want you to LISTEN to them."

"Okay," I said. Maybe I could figure that out later. Right now, I wanted as much information as I could get out of her. "So I read these snippets—"

"One a day—"

"And I listen to what they're telling me."

"Just listen to them."

"Okay. What else do I listen to?"

"Pay attention to the God-wonders. All around you."

"You mean like nature?"

"That's part of it."

"Everything is part of it!"

She smiled. "Now you're getting it."

"I'm not!"

"Look for the God-wonders. There's a huge stockpile of them. Then listen to the pictures they give you. You see everything in pictures, so that shouldn't be hard for you."

Hard? I was feeling like this was impossible. *I'm not some kind of mystic, lady!* I wanted to say. And yet, I didn't really want to say it, or I probably would have by then. I just gave her a bewildered look, and she put her hand over mine.

"Don't let this become a task," she said. "Listening for God is almost like play. You get to be a kid with God, even when nobody else will let you be one anymore. Enjoy looking for the ways God blesses you."

"IS He blessing me right now?" I said. "Because if he is, I think I'm missing something."

"I think you are too, and that's tragic, because, do you know what a blessing is, Laura?"

"I don't think I know anything for sure," I said.

"Know this," she said. Her eyes were glowing again. "Blessing is the imparting of supernatural favor. It's the wonderful, unlimited goodness that only God has the power to know about or GIVE to us. It's beautiful."

"But what about MY power?" I said. "I mean, you said you were going to give me the key to having—what did you call it—secret power?"

"Your power is in God's grace." She pulled back to survey me. "You look a little disappointed."

"I just had a different image," I said. "I'm sorry."

"Don't be sorry," she said. "You'll get it. Meanwhile, look at it this way: if you want the illusion that you have control, just watch what God is doing and follow that."

"But how do I know what he's doing?"

She smiled slowly, almost slyly. "You listen," she said.

"And I'll hear? Guaranteed?"

"If you're making yourself available by paying attention to the blessings and listening to the Word—and finding the quiet. We didn't get to that part yet. You need to find space and time to be alone and quiet."

I groaned. "At my house? Good luck."

"Oh, honey," she said. "Luck has absolutely nothing to do with it. God will provide your quiet places, but you have to be paying attention. And when you do all these things, God will open your ears so you CAN listen, and the Word will enter your life and become part of your very being, and you will have the power of surrender."

I at least knew what she meant by passion now, because I was seeing it in the light in her eyes and hearing it in the pictures she was creating with her warm voice. I wanted that passion too. I wanted that power.

I just couldn't believe I was going to get it the way she said I was going to get it.

I smiled, though, as I took the piece of paper on which she had written "Psalm 62," and I continued to smile as she told me to read only a few verses a day and chew on them as if they were delicious morsels from God. I nodded when she told me that it was going to take a while for me to be able to get perfectly quiet and distinguish God's voice from my own thoughts, and that the answers God was going to give me were going to come in surprising forms, at least from her experience.

But my heart wasn't entirely in it, and, of course, she knew it. As I started to stand up, she said in the softest, warmest voice yet, "One more thing, Laura. Answer a question for me."

I could give her that. I had to.

"Who do you think Jesus is?" she said.

"He was the Son of God," I said, sounding just like a computer-generated telephone operator. So I added quickly, "I do believe that. He was God in human form, and he came down to leave us the message in the Gospels that shows us how to live, and to save us from our sins, and to die so we can have eternal life."

"Very correct," she said. "But if you want the power of what that all means to you NOW, take a chance: If you dare, Laura, stay in this sacred space where you are and hear God."

Then she got up and left me sitting there. I wasn't sure, but I thought she was about to cry. The next day, I got a note from her, delivered to my homeroom.

She'd written:

> *I forgot to tell you that things could get scary and confusing. I'll be here for you.*

Too late, I thought as I folded up the note and stuck it into my backpack. *I'm already scared and confused.*

And that was because I HAD tried her little techniques the night before.

It had been pointless to attempt any quiet time until after Bonnie went to bed and my homework was done, which put me at about ten o'clock.

As for space, my room had to be it, and that wasn't exactly a place where I figured God wanted to hang out. I didn't even like hanging out in there. That was mostly because I hadn't done anything to fix it up since we'd moved in. There were still boxes waiting around to be unpacked, full of posters from musicals I'd been in and scrapbooks that contained every piece of my former life, right down to the wrapper from the roll of Lifesavers the soprano section had shared backstage at my last concert. I knew I wouldn't be able to look at any of it without either crying hysterically or pelting something through my window. I hadn't even unpacked my computer because that would lead to email from friends back home and would only highlight my homesickness.

With everything I cared about still in boxes, the walls were bare, stark white except for the copy of my class schedule, which I'd taped just above my desk so I could do a mental checklist of homework every night. It wasn't what I would call a sacred space.

But it was all I had, so I turned out the glaring overhead light and stretched out on the bedspread my mother had forced me to pick out, to the tune of, "Laura, you cannot live like a monk. Let's at least put a comforter on your bed."

It was far from comforting as I lay there, trying to hear God.

At first, all I heard were the house sounds. The drippy faucet my father had tried four times to fix. The icemaker in the kitchen spitting cubes into their container. The fish tank in the den, giving life support to fish no one ever looked at. I even listened for signs of life from my goldfish, Beethoven, in the small bowl on my dresser. There shouldn't be any. I'd forgotten to feed him three days in a row. The fish thrived on neglect.

Listen for the God-wonders, Mrs. Isaacsen had said. I was sure the fact that Beethoven was still alive was not the kind of thing she was talking about.

I churned restlessly to my side and tried closing my eyes. Maybe the stuff I was supposed to be hearing was on the inside. There was always plenty to listen to in MY head.

My brain didn't disappoint me. It was so noisy in there, I could barely distinguish one whining, screaming, wailing voice from another. A few did manage to make themselves heard.

Congratulations! You've transformed yourself from a winner into a loser in a few short weeks. Maybe you should start teaching a course on it.

Nah. You were never a winner in the first place or you wouldn't have lost it so easily. Who did you think you were, anyway?

Hear God? Uh, I don't think so.

I sat straight up in bed. My heart was beating so hard I put my hand on my chest to make sure it wasn't pounding its way out. Breathing like a westbound train, I stumbled from the bed and fumbled for the light switch. When the room sprang into a glare again, I saw my hands, shaking and glistening with sweat, clinging to the wall.

I did unpack one of the boxes then—the one that had my TV in it. The rabbit ears didn't bring in much besides snow, but at least it was noise. It was the drone of *Friends* reruns that finally lulled me off to sleep, long after midnight.

After about four nights of dozing off with David Letterman or Jay Leno or infomercials about liposuction, it became a habit. I didn't really listen to it. I just let it cover the God-less silence I couldn't stand.

I did try to find other quiet times and places, I really did. We were still on the end of Daylight Savings Time that last week in October, so when Mom got home a little early one evening, I asked if I could go for a walk.

"Is she getting to you?" she whispered to me.

"Who?" I said.

"Your sister. You know, you don't have to play with her all the time, Laura. You CAN park her in front of the TV once in a while, as long as it's something she's allowed to watch."

I didn't have the guts to tell her I did that every day.

It was probably time I got out into the neighborhood a little anyway, I thought. Bonnie was starting to bug me about going to the park, and I didn't even know where there was one. Up until now, I'd been too stubborn to care what existed outside the walls of our house. But now I had two reasons: the park and a quiet place for me in daylight.

Actually, I hoped I'd find the first and not the second. The whole idea of quiet was scaring me more every night.

Our house, which I realized early on was probably the only pink stucco one in the Cove, was just two blocks from St. Andrew's Bay, a fact Dad had been advertising to us since the day he'd put in the offer on the place. The route down to it was lined with tall pines and live oaks hung with that strange Spanish moss that looked like old men's beards. It reminded me of the Amish men we used to see at home, driving their buggies down the farm roads.

Here and there, I saw a shorter palm splaying its fronds out over a yard, or a line of tall palms trying to create the illusion that we were in some tropical paradise. It was a funky juxtaposition: palm trees in yards and wreaths of autumn leaves on doors.

Actually, though, it WAS tropical compared to where I came from. Here the hydrangeas and the azalea bushes grew up past people's windows, and some of those still clung to their faded blossoms. There were ferns and succulents growing around mailboxes that I had only seen as houseplants in Missouri. Although the occasional acorn snapped under my feet as I walked, I wasn't all together sure it wasn't spring and not autumn. Only the Halloween ghosts, witches, and goblins tied to trees and porch railings told me otherwise.

The road came to a dead end at Bunker's Cove Road where Dad said the bay was. I could see it ahead of me, barely. Most of it was screened by a large sign that read:

YACHT CLUB
PRIVATE

"Fine," I muttered to it. "I don't want to belong to your stupid old club anyway."

I knew I sounded like Bonnie, who called everything of mine
stupid or *old* when I wouldn't let her play with it. My walk down
Bunker's Cove Road did nothing to change my attitude.

I couldn't even SEE the bay, much less get down to it. Every inch
of the coastline was owned by somebody with a mansion, a tennis
court, and an in-ground swimming pool. I was almost ready to
turn around in disgust when I spotted an empty lot that was for
sale. I ran to its edge like a kid chasing the Good Humor truck, just
so I could get a glimpse of what everyone was shutting me off
from.

I wasn't disappointed. For a good five minutes, I stood staring
down at water so blue it nearly made my eyes ache. There was just
enough breeze to chop it into tiny white caps, enough to set the
pampas grass in motion and get the comical palms swaying. It was
mesmerizing, and I wanted to stretch out on the grass and let it lull
me out of the anxious buzz I was living with.

But it was still somebody else's property. The FOR SALE sign
announced that clearly. This wasn't MY quiet place because I didn't
belong here. I didn't belong anywhere.

That night I tried listening to music instead of the TV. I'd told
Mrs. Isaacsen it was music that had led me to really believe in
Christ in the first place. Back in Missouri, there was hardly a time
when I didn't have some kind of tunes going.

I'd always had the radio on in the bathroom when I was taking a
shower.

I'd always played CDs while doing my homework.

The minute I got into the car with Mom I'd always turn on the
stereo, and I didn't even mind that she insisted on listening to the
Oldies station. I knew every word to every song, even when she
didn't. "How do you DO that?" she used to say to me.

I used to sit at the piano for hours practicing choir music. And
when we had auditions coming up, all my friends would come
over, and we'd help each other with our pieces, even though we
were all competing for the same parts. When they left, I was
usually so wired, I'd sit there plunking out my own songs as they
curled around in my head like wisps of smoke, until Dad would
tell me he was piano-ed out for the day.

I had loved it all—operas on TV, Broadway musicals on my
mom's old records, gospel choirs on early Sunday morning radio.
Hip-Hop. R&B. Country Western. Pop. Rock. Even some alterna-
tive rock. Everything but rap was something I could sing to, move
to, think to. A good song had coaxed me out of many a crazy tree.

But now I couldn't even stand hearing the muffled sounds of
Bonnie's *Veggie Tales* tapes in the next room. I hadn't even opened
the keyboard cover on the piano since the movers had parked it in
the living room. All it took was one bar, one scrap of a melody and
I was aching all over, missing Missouri. I would have been in the
jazz choir and the advanced ensemble. The music department was
doing *Grease* this season, and I'd had a real shot at playing Sandy,
even though I was only a junior. I'd even been willing to dye my
hair blonde . . .

So it didn't work that night when I put in my *Grease* CD and
tried to get quiet. Half-way through "You're the One that I Want" I
was bawling. I shut it off and felt myself floundering.

Okay, one thing I hadn't tried was Mrs. Isaacsen's snippets. I'd
read Psalm 62 the day she gave it to me, but it hadn't done much
for me. Yeah, of course she'd said to read just a few verses at a
time, but when it came to studying, my experience had been that
more was always better.

But then, she'd said not to study it.

I sighed and pulled my Bible out of the drawer in my bedside
table and flipped to Psalm 62.

All right, I thought. *I'll close my eyes, point my finger, and read whatever my finger lands on.*

The first thing I saw when I opened my eyes was that my fingernail was bitten down to the quick. Matter of fact, they all were.
When had that happened? I'd always been a stress queen, but I'd
never hit cuticle. It was pretty hard to gnaw your nails when you
had braces.

Okay, back to the psalm. I lifted my finger as if the verse was
going to jump off the page and into my face, and I read: *For God
alone my soul in silence waits.*

My eyes slammed shut again, and so did the Bible. *I'm waiting!* I
thought. *I'm alone and I'm silent and I'm waiting—so where are you?
Where ARE you?*

There was no answer. There was only the buzzing of fear at
every nerve ending, and I couldn't stand it.

I grabbed the remote and switched on the TV, hoping the drone
would lull me to sleep. No luck.

I propped myself up in bed and started clicking.

There were no God wonders. There were women, my age and a
little older, flirting with guys, fighting off guys, giving guys mixed
signals, dressing for guys, undressing for guys . . .

I flipped faster and harder, but that was all I could see, until I was sure every station was showing the same program. I felt dizzy and dirty and somehow sucked in.

This is the world Mrs. Isaacsen was talking about, I thought. *But it's the world I have to fit into if I'm going to have any power at all.*

I tried, Mrs. I. I really tried.

I only got four hours sleep that night, and it was pretty obvious when I looked in the mirror the next morning that I was going to have to do something about those bags under my eyes. They looked like carry-on luggage.

As I reached for the concealer, I had an idea. If I had no choice but to fit into the world I was being presented with, I was going to have to start by at least LOOKING like I fit in.

I used a half a tube of concealer, all the rest of my liquid foundation, and a bunch of the blush I hadn't used since *Oklahoma*. I didn't own any eye shadow, but my mom's eyebrow pencil gave me the same smudged-eyeliner effect I'd seen on Celeste when she was going for the Material Girl thing one day. A little lip gloss – okay, a lot of lip gloss – and I felt like I was getting there.

From the closet I selected a pair of jeans that were not falling off of me, as most of mine were by then, and rolled them down to my hipbones. I tried getting one of my smaller hoop earrings to stay in my belly button somehow but all THAT did was dig up belly button dust. It was against dress code to show your midriff anyway, and wanting to avoid ending up in Mr. Stennis's office yet again, I opted for a long white stretch top that practically covered my rear end. At least I *felt* a little powerful.

It wasn't hard to get past Mom. She was still nursing her first cup of coffee as I sailed through the kitchen and tossed a good-bye over my shoulder. But I didn't get past Celeste.

I ran into her in the locker area before school, and she took one look at me and hauled me off to the bathroom.

"What's with the make-up?" she said as she dug into a beaded handbag and pulled out a package of Wet Ones. She was going for the glamour look that day. "Did you put it on with a putty knife or what?" she said.

"I was trying to look more sophisticated," I said.

I stood there, feeling completely powerless as she went after my face.

"You're lookin' a little bit like that TV evangelist with the pink hair," she said. Then she stopped wiping and stepped back to look at me. "That's better. You do look good in SOME make-up. I like it." Her eyes took on a sly gleam. "So will Richard."

"Who's Richard?" I said.

"The guy you're going to hook up with. He doesn't go here, so I've got it set up so you two can meet at the mall tomorrow. After school. You can make it, right?"

I was already shaking my head.

"Look, don't ditch me on this," she said. "I'm goin' with ya. It's not like a blind date."

"It's not that," I said. "I have to baby-sit my little sister every day after school."

"So bring her with."

"Right," I said. "Like my mother is going to go for that. You don't understand: if somebody besides me baby-sits her, they practically have to provide a blood sample. My mom is way protective."

Celeste was now going after my hair, fluffing it out with her fingers and spraying underneath it from a tiny vial of hairspray she had produced from the beaded handbag.

"I call this 'I Just Got Outa Bed, Aren't I Cute?'," she said. "Work on your mom. You don't wanna miss this character I got lined up for you. He's a Christian, the whole thing. He even tried to convert me once."

"I'll try," I said. I had to, or I felt like I was going to die.

But I knew chances were slim-to-none that my mother was going to let me take Bonnie to the Panama City Mall with Celeste, the Boy Magnet, so I could get hooked up with a guy. This Richard person could be an ordained pastor, but that wasn't going to matter to Mom.

Hopeless as it was, though, I mulled over it all day. I was still taking it apart and putting it back together in chemistry class when Mr. Frohm broke me out of it by calling me up to his desk.

"He's telling us our mid-term grades today," the red-haired girl next to me whispered. I'd learned from Mr. Frohm constantly calling on her that her name was Deidre. It was as if he was giving her every chance to have the right answer someday. "Good luck," she said.

I held my breath all the way up there and hoped he wouldn't somehow notice by chemical deduction that I had my jeans rolled down to my hip bones.

"Good news," he said to me. His bald head looked somehow shinier than usual. "I've got you a tutor."

"Are you serious?" I said.

A couple of the nerds glanced up at me curiously. I lowered my voice. "Is it that one guy?"

"Trent Newell," Mr. Frohm said. "I worked a deal: he'll tutor you and I'll give him special tutoring in advanced calculus since they aren't offering that here this semester."

I felt a groan coming on. I'd known that it was going to be a boy and that he was going to be smart, but advanced calculus? I was feeling stupider by the second.

But I couldn't go there. I really had to ace this class, or I could kiss my chances at a great scholarship to a number-one school good-bye.

"Your average right now is a C," Mr. Frohm said. "That's certainly nothing to be ashamed of."

Yeah? I thought as I picked my way through the backpacks and returned to my desk. *Then why am I about to put myself through more humiliation at the hands of a mathematical genius?*

As I sunk into my desk, I tried to replace the image of a disgusted senior trying to drag me through the periodic table with the picture of a big fat computer-printed A on my report card.

"Why are you worried about a C?" Deidre hissed from the seat next to me. "I'd kill for a C!"

Because my life is one big worry, I wanted to tell her. *Nothing but one big worry.*

chapter seven

I actually played with Bonnie that afternoon. We went through the
whole dress-up box about twelve times and put together a
Halloween costume for her. With funds low and Mom working,
she was still without an identity for the party at school the next
day. Trick-or-treating was out of the question because of the allergy
situation, but I wanted her to at least have the coolest costume in
her class.

There was that, and then there was the fact that if I spent one more
afternoon doing nothing, my own thoughts were going to drive me
nuts. Besides THAT, I wanted to feel self-righteous when I tried to
talk Mom into letting me take Bonnie to the mall the next day.

By the time Mom got home, I had Bonnie decked out as the most
magnificent angel since Gabriel himself. She'd wanted Raggedy
Ann, which I couldn't quite pull off, but when I put her in the
wings I'd fashioned from coat hangers and the netting from one of
my old choir gowns, all thoughts of anybody raggedy were extin-

guished. I thought she was going to try to take flight.

Mom came in, bent under huge bags of groceries, and stood there in the doorway, eyes tearing up. While Bonnie pirouetted for her and pointed out every flake of glitter I'd glued to the ensemble, I rushed to take the bags off Mom's hands. I poured her a Diet Coke on crushed ice and suggested that I fix dinner. She finally pulled the tears back, sent Bonnie off to change, and said, "All right, Laura, what do you want and how much is it going to cost me?"

It was a funny thing about my mom. She had this cherubic face, like a grown-up Bonnie, but she had the most sarcastic sense of humor. A lot of times it was pretty funny, actually, except when she was stressed out, and then it got snappy and sharp and bordered on mean. She'd been in THAT mode ever since Dad had lost his job seven months ago. She'd been unstressed for about an hour after he finally got employed again, and then she'd started stressing about moving—and then about getting settled—and then about finding a doctor for Bonnie and a job for herself . . .

Yeah, it had been a while since Mom had been funny.

"It's not gonna cost you a dime," I said. "All I want to do is go to the mall tomorrow afternoon with Celeste."

"And she is . . . ?"

"A friend of mine."

Mom froze, her hip still cocked to close the refrigerator door. "Did you say friend?" she said.

"Uh-huh."

She folded her arms. "All right, who are you and what have you done with my daughter?"

I rolled my eyes.

"My daughter, Laura Duffy—you may know her—was deter-mined not to make any friends here because she refused to resign herself to the fact that she no longer lives in Cameronville, Missouri."

"Celeste just started asking me to have lunch with her and now she wants to go to the mall together."

Mom did push the door shut then and looked a little sad. "I'm sorry, hon," she said. "There's no one else to watch Bonnie."

"We'll take her with us."

"Right. I've been to that mall, remember? It isn't a shopping center; it's a hang out. Two sixteen-year-old girls watching my six-year-old in that zoo? I don't think so."

I could feel the hair on the back of my neck standing up, and it

WAS righteous hair as far as I was concerned. "That's so not fair," I said. "You make it sound like I'm not responsible for Bonnie. I've never messed up when I'm taking care of her."

Mom stopped pelting apples into a basket to look at me. Her voice softened.

"I'm sorry," she said. "I know how you are about Bonnie. That was out of line."

I didn't say anything. It felt like maybe I was gaining some points and I didn't want to risk messing it up.

"You'd have to make sure she didn't eat anything she's not allowed to have," Mom said. "And she can't get too worked up. You'd have to keep her quiet. And you can't take your eyes off of her for a second. You know how fast she is. I wish she weren't too big for a stroller."

I couldn't stand it any longer. "So I can go and take her?"

"As long as I can meet this friend—what's her name?"

"Celeste!" I called over my shoulder. I was already on my way to the phone.

"My mom just wants to meet you is all," I told Celeste when I'd delivered the news.

"No problem," she said. "I'll be over in ten."

She was there in five, which gave me zero time to prepare Mom for what Celeste was going to be like. It had all happened so fast; it hadn't occurred to me until I'd hung up the phone that Mom meeting Celeste could actually be the demise of this whole plan. By then she was practically pulling into our driveway – in an old car that appeared to have been fixed up by somebody and fitted with a large set of woofers and tweeters. The thing was vibrating U-2 all the way down the block.

I went out to meet her and only had enough time to whisper, "I didn't tell my mom I was meeting a guy," before Bonnie, too, bolted out of the front door and planted herself in front of Celeste.

"Gotcha," Celeste murmured back to me and then stooped down to face Bonnie.

"You are like this little doll baby," Celeste said.

"I'm six," Bonnie said, holding up the appropriate number of fingers.

"No stinkin' way," Celeste said.

"Yes, way," Bonnie said.

"Can ya prove it?"

Bonnie was only puzzled for about a half a second. Then she shot her blue eyes up at me and said, "Tell her how old I am, Laurie."

"Man, has she got you wrapped," Celeste said to me.

The surprising thing was that in minutes, Bonnie had Celeste wrapped around HER little finger. I hadn't figured Celeste for the kid-loving type, but she had Bonnie dragging out every Barbie known to womankind and was dressing them in combinations of clothes that only Celeste could dream up. Biker Barbie was my personal favorite. Bonnie was charmed.

So was Mom. She took one look at Celeste sitting on the floor playing Barbies with Bonnie and she immediately invited her for dinner.

"Laura's dad's working late," Mom said, "so it'll be just us girls."

That was kind of what I was afraid of: Celeste getting cozy with "us girls" and detailing her Adventures WITH Boys. But either Celeste was being on her best behavior, or she had had a personality transplant on the way over from her place, because she scarfed down two bowls of Mom's beef stew, complimented Mom on how beautiful our house was, and laughed at all of Mom's un-funny jokes. Celeste seemed to de-stress Mom like a two-hour Calgon bath. Mom even got Bonnie into HER bath early and then served us dessert in the family room so we could "chat."

I was starting to feel a little too much togetherness with "us girls," but Celeste didn't seem to mind it at all. In fact, she tucked her feet up under her on the couch and savored both the apple crisp and Mom's questions like they were equally delicious.

"What does your dad do?" Mom said.

"He's a gearhead," Celeste said.

"Excuse me?" Mom said.

"He works on cars. He has a shop on 231 and he works at home on the ones he races. We have like 20 of them in our yard."

"I've been looking for a good mechanic. My van sounds like it's constipated."

I stifled a groan. Celeste gave an appreciative grunt.

"And what about your mother?" Mom said. "Does she work?"

"I don't know," Celeste said. "She doesn't live with us. You don't mind if I put a little more whipped cream on this, do you? She moved out when I was like two. My dad kicked her out, if you wanna know the truth. He came home one night and she was doin' a line of cocaine right next to my playpen. He said he wouldn't call the cops if she'd pack up and get out and never try to get custody of me."

"I'm so sorry," Mom said.

"Yeah," I said. I was beyond sorry. I was in shock.

"So you've basically grown up without a mother?" Mom said.

"I had my grandmother 'til we moved down here when I was a freshman." Celeste gave her usual cheerful smile as she added a third squirt out of the whipped cream can. "It was probably a good thing we moved when we did. She and I were starting to get into some fights about stuff like make-up and boys. I think she was hoping I'd become a nun."

I almost choked.

"And she would think that because—?" Mom said.

"She raised me Catholic—you know, the rosaries, the First Communion in the white dress, the whole thing. I was, like, way into it, 'til I hit puberty. Then I started asking some questions, you know what I'm saying?"

"I know what you're saying," Mom said.

I wasn't sure I did, but I wasn't going to pursue it either. So far, things were going well. In fact, Mom looked like she wanted to adopt Celeste, and I didn't want to risk her finding out what a boy fiend Celeste was, although it wouldn't have surprised me if Mom had chosen to overlook that fact. I'd almost forgotten about it myself.

"So you girls are going to the mall tomorrow, I hear," Mom said—as if there had never been any discussion to the contrary.

"I thought I'd take Laura shopping, show her where everybody buys their clothes," Celeste said. "Not that she doesn't have a gorgeous wardrobe. She's like the best-dressed girl in school. I should HAVE the clothes she has."

I wasn't sure what to think first. *I am SO not the best-dressed girl in school. If you had my clothes, Celeste, you'd still turn them all into costumes.* Or, *I feel SO guilty not telling Mom that we're not going to the mall to go shopping.*

When Mom left me twenty dollars in an envelope on the kitchen table the next morning with a note that said, *Buy yourself something nice. You deserve it,* I almost ran out the door after her and confessed the whole thing. Making a vow to myself to come clean that night, I went to my room to figure out what out of my "gorgeous wardrobe" I was going to wear to impress this Richard guy.

I started with a dress, but that looked like I was going on a date – too eager—so I ditched it for my Abercrombie and Fitch sweater, but that seemed like I was trying to impress him with labels, so I went for a pair of bell bottoms Mom had made me, only I was afraid it would seem like I was homespun—

By the time it was five minutes before I was supposed to leave

for the bus, I was standing in the middle of my room, in my under-
wear, with ten different outfits sprawled everywhere.

What is my deal anyway? I thought as I grabbed my carpenter
jeans out of the closet. *This guy isn't going to want to date me anyway,
so what am I worried about?*

I wriggled into a black top, stuck my hair in a ponytail, and
dashed for the bus.

Celeste met me at my locker, face shining like she was the maid
of honor.

"Look at you!" she said.

"I couldn't find anything to wear."

"No, you're perfect. " She stepped back from me, hands up in a
square like she was looking through a camera lens. "Understated.
Mysterious. He's gonna flip out, this guy."

"Right," I said.

She sighed. "We have SO gotta work on your self-esteem issues."

I tried to put "Richard" out of my mind the rest of the day, but I
wasn't very successful. When a guy showed up at my first period
English class with a note saying he was supposed to talk to me, I
thought it was HIM. After he told me his name was Trent Newell, I
stared at him stupidly in the hall for a full fifteen seconds before I
realized he was my chemistry tutor.

"Mr. Frohm sent me," he said.

"O-oh," I said. "Yeah."

And then we stood there gaping at each other. One thing was
perfectly clear—he was the only human being I had ever met who
was more awkward around a girl than I was around a boy.

He was a big kid, though not athletic-looking no matter how
far you stretched it. I had to tilt my head back to look up at
him, but he was kind of mushy. Not fat, just no muscles to flex
while standing at the water fountain. He had a couple of
pimples. Who didn't? But he had that painful look on his face
as if he were wishing disfiguring acne away with every breath.
Maybe it was the fact that his mouth was kind of too small for a
guy his size, or the situation with the contact lenses that were
making his eyes bloodshot. In either case, he just couldn't seem
to bring himself to look at me and kept his gaze locked firmly
on a point six inches above my head.

Celeste would have been having a fit over his hair. It was dark
and he had it cut short the way a lot of guys did, only he obviously
didn't know how to style it so his 'do was reminiscent of some of
the first-graders in Bonnie's class. That only added to his overall

state of bewilderment. I felt so bad for him, I actually took charge of the conversation.

"So—you're going to tutor me, right?" I said.

"Uh-huh."

"When do we start?"

"I don't know."

"Tomorrow?"

"Can't."

It was like playing a game of Twenty Questions, but I finally got it out of him that we could meet in the library during the activity period on the days I didn't have my Group. He evidently didn't have activities either, and I could see why. I wasn't sure he could speak more than a word at a time.

As he skulked off down the hall, I could feel my heart sinking. I wasn't holding out much hope for my chemistry grade with poor Trent tutoring me. He couldn't even look at me, much less talk to me.

It was a depressing thought. But then, at that point, what wasn't?

chaptereight

We had Group that day, which took my mind off of my upcoming and sure-to-be-doomed meeting with Richard the Christian. At least for a while.

Mrs. Isaacsen asked each of us to think of a situation when we'd been particularly vulnerable. Joy Beth and K.J. , I noticed, both frowned as if they were going to have to make something up to complete this assignment. I, on the other hand, had trouble deciding which ONE of my more shining moments to use.

"Who's willing to go first?" Mrs. Isaacsen said.

I was sure I LOOKED the most vulnerable, so I raised my hand. I told the group what had happened with Shayla in the counseling suite the week before. Even as I was describing Shayla poking her finger into my chest, my hands started to sweat. I sat on them so K.J. wouldn't see them shaking.

"I'd be watching my back if I were you," Joy Beth said when I was finished.

"Do I hear a question in there anywhere, Joy Beth?" Mrs. Isaacsen said.

"Sorry," Joy Beth said.

Mrs. Isaacsen turned back to me. "Now, Laura, I want you to imagine the scene again, only this time, I want you to picture yourself having some power and using it."

"AK47, anyone?" K.J. muttered.

I closed my eyes and saw myself, as clearly as if it had just happened, sitting on that bench, back plastered to the wall, as Shayla appeared out of nowhere and leaned over me.

"She goes, 'Do you LIVE at the office?'" I said. "And I go, 'Do YOU? You're here every time I'm here.'"

I opened my eyes to peek at Mrs. Isaacsen. She nodded for me to go on.

"Then she keeps looking down at me and her face is all, like distorted, and then she goes, 'You! YOU did this!' And then I stand up and I get all up in her face and I go, 'You did it to yourself, Shayla. And it wasn't the first time, so don't go blaming it all on me.'" I shrugged. "And then before she has a chance to say anything else, I get up and walk away."

"And then she body slams you to the floor!" K.J. said. Everyone laughed, except me.

"I don't think so," Mrs. Isaacsen said. "I think somebody like Shayla would be set back on her heels by that kind of confidence."

"So why can't you just do that next time she starts talkin' trash to ya?" Joy Beth said to me.

"Because I'm a wimp!" I said.

Even K.J. laughed at that. Not surprisingly, Michelle kept a straight face.

"I know we're just supposed to tell our own story," she said. "So I'm going to tell this because I think it could help."

"That's within the guidelines," Mrs. Isaacsen said. "Go ahead, Michelle."

Michelle sat up straighter and smoothed her skirt with her hands like they were little irons. "In my situation," she said, "I got to act like I'm older sometimes. I got people looking at me like, 'Who is THIS girl?' and I got to make them listen, so I just pretend I'm twenty-one or however old I got to be. In my situation, I've got to make them listen, so I always act as old as I can."

"Does it work?" Celeste said.

Michelle gave her an are-you-kidding look and in a high-pitched voice said, "Yea-ah!"

"What did you mean about your situation?" K.J. said.

My mind raced through several "situations" she might have to deal with.

Michelle folded her arms and seemed to fold herself inside at the same time. "Do I have to answer that?" she said.

"No, you do not," Mrs. Isaacsen said. "Not until you're ready. Who's next?"

Celeste volunteered next and proceeded to tell about the previous weekend when she "got with" a guy she wasn't interested in dating and then she ran into him at the Books-A-Million coffee shop the next day and had a major case of "post-hook-up anxiety."

The unknowns in that broke me out into a cold sweat. What did she mean by "got with"?

Maybe Michelle's right, I thought. *Maybe if I just acted like I knew what I was doing around this Christian boy, he'd think I actually did. I took over with Trent, didn't I, and acted all confident?*

Like THAT was a big accomplishment. Still, it might be worth a try—AFTER I told Celeste I had no intention of "getting with" this guy Richard, whatever that actually meant anyway. Good grief, I didn't even know the language. For me dating was a foreign country, and I decided to turn in my passport.

I started to go into that subject with Celeste in her car after school, but she immediately waved me off and said, "I know what kinda girl you are, all right? I'm not settin' you up for some one-night stand. We're talkin' serious here—long-term relationship. There's no other kind for you."

"I haven't even met the guy!" I said. "What if he hates me?"

"No stinkin' way," Celeste said. "You guys are perfect for each other. What school's your sister at?"

I gave her directions and tried to sit back and take some deep breaths. "Hey," I said, "This is a Mercedes."

"1984," Celeste said proudly. "My father fixed it up for me. Once in a while it's good to have a gearhead in the family, if you don't mind oil pans drainin' in the bathtub."

"I don't get it," I said. "If you drive this to school every day, how come you don't leave campus for lunch?"

"Because I hate hangin' out with that crowd that goes to the mall," she said. "They think I'm weird. I don't need it, y'know?"

"You? Weird?" I said.

"I don't do my shopping at Express. I don't pay twenty bucks to have my bangs trimmed. I don't sleep with middle linebackers. I don't sleep with anybody."

THAT was a huge relief. Now I felt guilty ever thinking she did.

"I like guys," Celeste said. "The cool ones stay at school for lunch, the ones that don't have egos bigger than Manhattan, you know what I'm sayin'? Hey, there's our kid!"

Her face lit up when she saw Bonnie standing in front of the school with her little class line, and from then on it was all about Bonnie. Celeste actually seemed to revel in the fact that Bonnie jacked her jaws nonstop from the time she climbed into the car until we stepped inside the mall. While Celeste was gooing and cooing over Bonnie's every syllable, I was wondering how I was going to keep Bonnie from telling Mom that Celeste had taken me there so I could meet a boy. But Celeste had that one neatly figured out.

We managed to get through the food court with promises to Bonnie that we would get her a snack on the way out and had just rounded the corner, so we had the fountain in sight, when Celeste cried, "Hey, there's a friend of mine!"

"Where's your friend?" Bonnie said.

"Right there. I've gotta go say hello to him."

Celeste grabbed Bonnie's hand and started for the fountain. Over the top of Bonnie's head, she gave me a brilliant smile and mouthed, "It's him."

Suddenly, I felt as if I were going in slow motion. My steps went long and deliberate and my ponytail seemed to hang in mid air with every bounce as I approached the fountain and the long-legged boy with hair tousled over his forehead and muscled arms hanging lazily from the sleeves of his polo shirt and a big smile—that sparkled with a mouthful of braces.

I almost laughed out loud. It was so vintage Celeste I could have hugged her. Instead, I smiled myself. At least that was one thing I didn't have to feel self-conscious about. Richard the Christian had twice as much orthodontia as I did. Now all I had to do was pretend I knew what I was going to do with it.

"Celeste!" the guy said as Celeste reached him and flung her arms around his neck. Bonnie hung shyly behind her. I knew that would last about seven seconds.

"This is a surprise," Celeste said. "What's up?"

"Just hangin' out," Richard said.

He had just a touch of a Southern accent lazing around his words like a sleepy bee at the honeysuckle. Or something. It definitely made pictures come to my head of fishing and taking naps in haystacks and going to the local diner for a Coke. It made me homesick.

"This is my pal Bonnie," Celeste was saying.

"She was surprised when she saw YOU," Bonnie said. She pointed a dimpled finger at Richard.

Celeste winked at me. Bonnie was sold, and now I didn't have to tell a lie to my parents. I liked Celeste more all the time.

Of course, I had kind of told a lie already, by leaving out this one important detail with Mom. Why couldn't anything just be clear anymore?

"And this is Laura," Celeste said.

I shook myself out of the internal debate I was having and flashed Richard another tinsel-toothed smile. He grinned back.

"Who's your orthodontist?" he said.

"Johnson," I said.

"Newton," he said.

"I'm glad we got that cleared up," Celeste said. "You want to walk around with us, Rich?"

"Sure," Richard said, as if that hadn't been the plan all along. It occurred to me that that could have been his opportunity to back out if it had been nausea at first sight.

Decision: I would think he was staying because he wanted to. It gave me enough confidence to say, "What school do you go to?"

"Moseley," he said.

"So how do you know Celeste?"

So far, acting "as if" was working. It was kind of like being in a musical, except we didn't break into a tap dance in front of J.C. Penney.

Richard grinned and fell into step beside me. "Who DOESN'T know Celeste? We both worked at Wendy's this summer. She's the only reason I stayed there longer than about a day. Everybody else would come in all hatin' life and she'd show up and everybody'd suddenly be laughing."

"Yeah," I said. "She does that to people."

I was beginning to wonder if Richard's decision to stay and hang out with us was because he liked Celeste so much, when he put his hands lazily into his pockets and said, "Celeste says you just moved down from Missouri. Is it hard making friends here?"

My throat immediately started to close up. Was it possible that somebody my own age actually cared how I felt about being the new kid? His eyes were so kind, I knew I was about to cry.

Celeste had definitely gotten it right. He was as nice to me as the guys back in my youth group, maybe even nicer. But crying wasn't part of the image I was trying to portray. I swallowed and said, "Yeah, it's way hard. Celeste has been great, but it's totally different here."

"Dude, and you're a junior," Richard said. "That's like the worst."

It seemed okay to launch into a tale of all my nightmares since I'd moved to P.C. To my surprise, he hung onto every word and laughed like I was doing a stand-up comedy routine. Yeah, this was definitely working. Pretend you're in control and, wow, you are.

"Hey, you want Baskin Robbins?" he said. "My treat."

I nodded and then looked around for Celeste and Bonnie. They were several stores behind us, examining a velour pant suit in Bonnie's size that my mother would say made kindergartners look like Britney Spears.

"Hey, who wants ice cream?" Richard called to them.

Bonnie was in his arms in a flash. I was convinced at that moment that my little sister was never going to have the kinds of issues with boys that I had.

The Baskin Robbins only had tables for two, and once Celeste and Bonnie had their ice cream, which Celeste made sure they got first, the two of them settled in at a table by themselves.

"Find your own table," Celeste said to Richard and me. "We're bonding."

"You only have vanilla, right?" I said to Bonnie.

"Yes. I'm not a-lergic to it," she said. "It doesn't have any bananas or chocolate or—"

"Geez, what do you live on?" Celeste said to her.

"Soy," Bonnie said immediately. "And vega-bles and—"

I left them to that conversation. I already had the list memorized.

Richard was by then setting our cappuccino blasts on our table. Then he even held the chair out for me to sit down. Okay, so it was a little much, but I was eating it up. So was he, because he kept grinning at me.

"Okay, confession," he said.

Uh-oh, I thought. *Here it comes. He's going to tell me he already has a girlfriend or something.*

"I knew you were coming today," he said.

"Well, yeah, I know," I said.

"Yeah, but you don't know that I was prepared to jam out of here if I saw you from a distance and you were like most of Celeste's friends. I mean, she promised me you weren't, but—"

It occurred to me that I had never seen Celeste with other girls. She only hung out with guys, as far as I could tell. Guys and me.

"Was she right?" I said.

He grinned. "I'm still here, aren't I? I don't know, this is weird. It's like we click or something. You're a Christian, right?"

"Yeah," I said. "Did Celeste tell you that I didn't want to meet a guy who wasn't?"

"She did. I was pretty impressed. I mean, a lot of girls say they won't go out with non-Christian guys but when it comes right down to it—" he shrugged.

I liked the way he didn't finish his sentences. It was like he didn't have everything all figured out and tied up into a neat little package. It was reassuring to know I wasn't the only one. Still, the trick was to pretend I did. And I felt like I was already getting pretty good at it.

"So do you have a church yet?" he said.

"No," I said.

"You should try my church. It's in Lynn Haven, but I could pick you up Sunday night. We have a pretty good youth group."

"That would be—cool," I said.

I wasn't sure, but I thought I might have been asked out on my first date. Well, maybe it wasn't a date. Probably better that it wasn't, since I wasn't sure what my parents were going to say. The subject of dating had never actually come up. I mean, why would it?

I started to ask Richard what time he'd be picking me up when a streak of Bonnie went by with Celeste on her heels.

"She's done with her ice cream—she's ready to move on," Celeste called out over her shoulder. She was still smiling.

Decision: I loved that girl. She was my new best friend.

"Guess we better walk," Richard said. "You're pretty cool with your little sister. Mine drives me nuts."

"How old is she?"

"Thirteen. She does that giggling thing that's like in some octave only dogs can hear. I hate that—"

"Laura!"

I reluctantly pulled my gaze away from Richard and looked ahead. Celeste was kneeling in front of Bonnie, her body tensed up like a piece of wire. Bonnie was leaning toward her, and she had both hands to her throat.

I took off toward them like a shot, letting my cup drop to the mall floor and roll away. I half-fell into Celeste as I slid on my knees in front of my sister. One look at her panicked little face, one sound of the gasps for air, and I knew what was happening.

She was having an allergic reaction. And it was the worst one I'd ever seen her have.

chapter nine

"What's going on?" Celeste said. "Is she choking?"

I didn't answer her. I just pulled Bonnie close to me and held her tight against my chest.

"It's okay, baby," I said. "Just try to calm down. I've got your medicine in my bag—"

Which was in the car.

"Go get my backpack!" I said to Celeste. "She's having a reaction and she needs her meds!"

Celeste sprang up, but Richard grabbed her arm. "I think you better get security," he said. "She's not breathing."

I pushed Bonnie out at arm's length and felt every one of my own vital functions stop. Her face was turning blue, and her eyes were drifting, as if we were losing her. I shook her, but I only felt her going limp in my hands.

"Go!" Richard shouted at Celeste.

She took off, screaming, "Somebody help us!" at the top of her lungs. Richard took Bonnie from me and laid her on the floor. I watched in stricken horror as he stuck his finger in her mouth

"What are you doing!"? I said.

I tried to push him out of the way but he brushed me off and put his mouth over Bonnie's. Her chest rose, but I knew he was doing the breathing for her. All I could do was rock back and forth and say over and over, "God, help! Please help! Please help!"

I kept saying it, in various degrees of panic, as a security guard arrived, took one look at the scene, and called for an ambulance. By then, we'd attracted a crowd. The guard took charge of keeping people from getting too close with their gawking, and a woman in scrubs pushed her way through and offered to relieve Richard. They took turns breathing for Bonnie until the paramedics arrived.

I was practically screaming at that point. Two of them got oxygen on Bonnie and lifted her like a rag doll onto a stretcher. One of them, a woman, came to me and wrapped a blanket around me, which I threw off as I tried to scramble up and go after my sister.

"We're going to Bay County Hospital," the woman said. "You kids have a car?"

"I'll bring her," Richard said.

"I want to be with Bonnie!" I shouted at all of them.

But the paramedics had already taken off at a dead run with the stretcher.

Somehow, we got into Richard's car, and I used Celeste's cell phone to call Mom at work. She and my dad showed up at the hospital only minutes after we arrived, but they charged past me and disappeared into the bowels of the emergency room, leaving me between Celeste, who was as pale and stiff as an icicle, and Richard, who put an arm around each of us and kept saying, "She's going to be fine. They've got her on oxygen."

"What just happened?" Celeste said. "I mean, we were just walkin' along talkin' and all of a sudden she stops and she goes, 'My tongue's getting big, Celeste.'" She rolled her eyes. "I thought she was playin', so I'm all stickin' my tongue out and the next thing you know, she's down on her knees gaggin'!"

"She was having an allergic reaction to something," I said. "But I only let her have vanilla ice cream. She can have that—"

"Can she have peanut butter?" Celeste said.

"No, that's the worst."

Celeste smacked her hand against her forehead and swore.

"What?" I said. "Celeste—WHAT?"

"I gave her some of my shake. It had those ground-up Reese's in it. I didn't know!"

I went for the door just as my father stepped out, his face as gray as his hair.

"Peanut butter!" I said to him.

He turned on his heel and disappeared again. I put my back to the wall and slid down until my tailbone hit the floor, and then I sat there with my face in my hands and sobbed.

I felt someone's fingers around my wrists, but I pulled away.

"Come over here and sit, Laura," Richard said. "You're going to get run over here."

"No!" I said. "She could die! Please, God, don't let her die!"

I sensed that he was sitting down on the floor beside me, and he stayed there while I cried myself hoarse. He only got up when I heard my mother say, "She's stabilized. Stand up, Laura."

I did, and I threw my arms around her neck. She held me, but I could feel the tension in her body.

"I'm so sorry, Mom," I sobbed into her shoulder. "It was an accident. Celeste didn't know about the peanut butter—"

"No, but you did. She went into anaphylactic shock." Mom pried me off of her and looked at me. Everything on her cherubic little face was coming to a point. "She can't live through too many more episodes like this. Do you get that? What were you thinking?"

"I didn't even see her drink it!"

"Did you think she was going to read the nutritional ingredients on the side of the package before she dug in?"

"It was my fault, Mrs. Duffy."

We all turned to look at Celeste, who was looking like a homeless waif at that point.

"She was getting antsy in Baskin Robbins and she'd already finished her ice cream, so I asked her if she wanted a sip of my milk shake. She asked if it were vanilla and I said yeah, with—but she didn't give me a chance to finish. She was gulping away." Celeste's face crumpled. "I shouldn't have even offered it to her. I feel horrible."

She sagged against Richard, who put his arm around her again.

"Who do I need to thank for giving her mouth-to-mouth?" Mom said.

"Richard," I said, pointing.

Mom stuck her hand out to shake his, and I saw that hers was trembling.

"Thank God you were there," she said to Richard. "You saved my baby's life."

Small red spots appeared in each of Richard's cheeks. "I learned it in a class I'm taking."

"Then thank God for the class," Mom said. "I wish there was something I could do for you."

"Nah," Richard said. He shrugged. "I was just there and I did it. Probably a God-thing."

Mom gave him a long look, and then she reached for Celeste. "I like your boyfriend," she said.

"He's not MY boyfriend," Celeste said. She sniffed noisily. I prayed she wouldn't add anything else to that statement.

Mom gave her a squeeze. "It wasn't your responsibility to know all of Bonnie's food allergies. I don't blame you. Just ask next time, huh?"

"I'm not giving her anything!" Celeste said. "She could beg me. I'd let her starve first! Can we go see her?"

"Yeah, I think they're almost finished with her down here," Mom said. "They're admitting her for overnight."

Celeste and Richard headed for the swinging door. I made a move to go after them, but Mom caught me by the arm.

"Do you understand the seriousness of what just happened?" she said when they were safely on the other side of the door.

"Yes! I take full responsibility for it, Mom. What else can I say? I am so, so sorry!"

I started to cry again. She pulled me to her shoulder, but her arms felt as if they were performing a duty. There was no comfort there. All I felt was the anxiety blazing through my veins, zinging to my heart, shooting into my lungs and squeezing them like bellows, zipping to my brain and telling it I was a horrible, disgusting, irresponsible, selfish person.

I was suddenly hot all over, and I could feel myself wanting to sink to the floor. That was ALL I needed to do right now, pass out and give my mother something else to stress about. The muscles in her arms already felt like bundles of telephone wire against my back.

I stepped away from her and tried to catch my breath.

"You coming in?" she said.

"In a minute," I said.

She nodded and left me there. I was still hugging myself and trying to breathe when Richard appeared through the doors.

"Are you okay?" he said.

"Yeah," I lied. "How's Bonnie?"

"She's in there runnin' her mouth." Richard grinned. "What does that tell ya?"

"She's fine."

"Yeah, but you're not." Richard put his finger under my chin and lifted it. THAT got my breathing going. "This really was an accident. Your mom's just upset."

"Yeah, I guess," I said.

"One good thing, though."

"What's that?"

"Since I gave your sister mouth-to-mouth, your mom'll probably let me pick you up Sunday night."

"Are you kidding?" I said. "She'll probably buy you a car!"

We laughed.

So there was the laugh with Richard, and that was good.

And I now had kind-of-a-date to look forward to.

And over the next few days, Bonnie recovered as if nothing had happened to her, though she did take full advantage of her convalescence. Mom took two days off and pampered her to death, and Celeste bought her about fifty bucks worth of Barbie clothes and spent a whole evening showing Bonnie how to turn them into a thousand different looks. Bonnie fell asleep clutching putty-nosed Barbra Streisand Barbie.

But none of that was enough to dispel the anxiety that constantly buzzed around in me like some out-of-control electrical short. A couple of times during those few days, I had those attack things again where my heart pounded so hard I felt like I couldn't breathe. It happened on Friday in study hall and I couldn't get it to stop. I asked for a pass to the counseling office.

Just knowing I was going to talk to Mrs. Isaacsen calmed me down. And by the time she was able to see me, I was okay. Well, relatively okay. I was back to baseline fear as opposed to full-blown panic.

"How's your sister?" she said.

"She's fine. You'd never know she almost died."

"Tea?"

I nodded and sank back into my comfort chair.

"And how about you?" Mrs. Isaacsen said. "Are you fine?"

I waited before I answered. I always liked to hear the hot water pouring into the cups. There was something soothing about it, like we were performing a familiar ritual.

"I guess I'm okay," I said. I didn't add, *At the moment.*

"How are things with Mom and Dad?"

"I don't know how they are with my dad," I said. I took the cup of Darjeeling she handed me and let it warm my palms. "The night

Bonnie was still in the hospital, he took me home and my mom stayed there; he said he forgave me for not being more 'vigilant' with Bonnie. Since then, he hasn't said anything to me. Of course, he's hardly ever with us, even for dinner."

"Still firing up the Skilsaw at the crack of dawn?" Mrs. Isaacsen said.

"Now it's a nail gun. He's putting hardwood floors in every-where."

"And Mother?"

I grunted, "I asked her if she forgave me and she said she did, but I can tell she's still mad at me. Everything I say to her, she snaps at me, and every day when she gets home I get, like, interro-gated about everything Bonnie ate and whether I watched her every second. I'm afraid to let her eat anything!"

"I can understand that," Mrs. Isaacsen said. "And I'm sure your mother feels the same way you do. She's just frightened."

I looked at her quickly. I hadn't actually revealed that I was scared out of my mind, had I? Saying I was "afraid" in that context shouldn't have given away that much.

She didn't follow up on it, though. She peeled a Post-It Note off the stack on the desk and picked up a pen.

"Has Psalm 62 told you everything it's going to tell you?" she said.

"'For God alone my soul in silence waits,'" I said.

She gave me a long look, but I couldn't read it.

"Listen to this one next," she said. "In snippets."

She wrote down Psalm 40 and handed me the sticky note. "Stay in your sacred, liminal space, Laura," she said. "Don't give in and slide backward. There's nothing there for you anymore."

The bell rang before I could ask her what that meant. I didn't like the sound of it, for sure. I knew if I went back to Missouri the next day, I'd be happy again.

That afternoon Bonnie fell asleep, which Mom told me—about thirty times—that she probably would because she'd had a shot that morning. The silence gave me too much space to think, and it was Friday and I knew I'd really feel like a geek if I started doing homework. So, with Bonnie snoozing on the couch where I could keep an eye on her, lest she should ingest something in her sleep, I got out the Bible and turned to Psalm 40. The one in the family room was *The Message*, which meant it was easy to read. I wasn't of course, going to limit myself to snippets. I was bent on reading the whole thing.

I waited and waited and waited for God.

THAT was the understatement of the millennium.

At last he looked; finally he listened.

Lucky for YOU. I'm still waiting.

> *He lifted me out of the ditch,*
> *Pulled me from deep mud.*
> *He stood me up on a solid rock*
> *To make sure I wouldn't slip.*
> *He taught me how to sing the latest God-song*
> *A praise-song to our God.*
> *More and more people are seeing this:*
> *They enter the mystery*
> *Abandoning themselves to God.*

At the moment, I wasn't seeing anything except the blur of the page on the other side of my tears. How come that wasn't happening to me? Why wasn't I being pulled out of this ditch and being taught the latest God-song? *What am I, God—chopped liver?*

I may very well have thrown *The Message* across the room if the phone hadn't rung. As it was, I let the book slip to the floor as I scrambled to answer it before it woke Bonnie up.

"Hey," said the voice on the other end. "This is Richard."

"Oh!" I said—eloquently. "Hi."

"How's our girl?" he said.

"Good. She's going to be okay."

"I coulda told you that."

Richard laughed just as lightly as he spoke. Too bad he was just calling to see how Bonnie was.

Decision: I liked him. And not because he was one of the few boys who had ever given me more than two minutes' notice. I liked his laugh and his braces and his accent and the fact that he knew how to save people's lives.

"So—am I still picking you up on Sunday?" he asked.

"Um, I think so," I said. My palms were starting to sweat. *Pretend control,* I told myself. *Pretend control.*

"You don't know for sure?" he said. He actually sounded disappointed.

"I haven't asked my parents yet. They aren't exactly thrilled with me."

"So does that mean they might not let you go to a party with me tomorrow? I mean, if you want to."

"A party?" I said. I'm surprised I didn't add, *Me?*

"Our youth group's having our last beach party before it gets too cold," he said. "Probably wouldn't be cold to you, but we're wimps here."

"Oh—a church party," I said. "They might. They'll want to know every detail, though." I grunted, rather attractively I might add. "Do you have a copy of your fingerprints?"

He laughed again. I seemed to have that effect on him.

"We're goin' to St. Andrew's State Park," he said. "About two— and we'll stay until after the bonfire, like eight o'clock or somethin'. I'll pick you up—we'll meet at the church—there will be, like, a hundred chaperones."

"How many kids are there?"

He snickered. "About thirty. I'm just kiddin'. There's like two adults for every ten kids and nobody goes wandering off in couples in the sand dunes or stuff like that."

Bummer, I thought. And then I mentally smacked myself and said, "I'll ask them. Can you call me back?"

"Why don't you call me?"

"They won't let me call a boy, even to get homework. They're a little out of it that way."

"I hear that," he said. "What time should I call?"

When we hung up, I still couldn't believe it was happening. I tried to tell myself he just wanted to get evangelism points for bringing me to youth group, and he was probably taking me so I could meet people, and I'd probably end up hanging out with girls who were being nice to me because I was new.

But none of that completely erased the vision of just walking along the sand with Richard. Only I didn't get too far with that visually because I'd never been to the beach. Ever. In my whole life. We didn't have them in Missouri—duh—and my parents hadn't had time to take us across the bridge to the Gulf since we'd been here. My few glimpses of the bay between houses hadn't been all that amazing. Maybe just being able to see the Gulf of Mexico would be enough.

Decision: I was really going to work on Mom—and Dad, too, if I had to—to let me go.

Huh. I barely had to say a word past, "Richard called." Mom went on and on about what a wonderful young man he was and why didn't I invite him over. All I had to say was, "He invited ME—" and she said yes. He could have been taking me to Las Vegas for all she knew.

She hurried into the family room at that point, picking her way around the boxes of nails and hardwood flooring, to check on Bonnie. She immediately started fluffing pillows and folding afghans and picking stuff up off the floor. She paused when she picked up *The Message*.

"What's this doing out?" she said.

"I was reading it," I said.

She looked at me out of narrowed eyes. "You have it BAD for this boy, don't you?" she said. "He's got you reading Scripture on a Friday afternoon."

"No, I don't have it BAD," I said, trying to keep any kind of "tone" out of my voice, lest my plans for tomorrow be parentally snuffed out. "I was reading it for another reason."

She didn't ask me what that was, because Bonnie sleepily opened her eyes, and Mom's sarcasm immediately melted away. I took that opportunity to escape to my room for daydreaming, with *The Message* in hand.

Okay, God, I thought, *so maybe you ARE pulling me out of the ditch.* I tried to snicker like Richard did. *He sure feels like solid rock to me!*

The next twenty hours were endless. I occupied myself with daydreaming about bonfires and sand dunes and a guy who laughed like pampas grass in the wind—and with choosing the right outfit. I finally gave up on that and called Celeste to come over. She was practically doing cartwheels as she went through every item of clothing I owned and packed my beach bag for me.

"Too bad you don't have a two piece," she said.

"Is it actually going to be warm enough to go swimming?" I said.

"No," she said. "You're right. 'Kay, but wear short sleeves and be sure to put on plenty of sun tan lotion. It'll make your arms soft in case he happens to brush up against you."

"No stinkin' way," I said. "He's taking me to a church thing. It's not like it's a date."

"Oh, yeah?" she said. Her sandy eyebrows went up. She reminded me of Mrs. Isaacsen. "Then why didn't he just wait for Sunday? Why didn't he just go tonight, have fun with his friends, and not have to worry about you having a good time? Why did he call me yesterday and ask me if I thought you'd go?"

I stared. "No, he did not."

"I do not lie about these things, my friend. I like barely got in the door yesterday and my phone was ringin' off the hook. He was VERY nervous, which is an excellent sign."

"He wasn't nervous!"

"Were you when he called you?"

"Yes!"

"Did you let on that you were?"

"No. I just pretended I was in control."

"Well, what do you think HE was doing? And he wouldn't be goin' through all this if he didn't like you—I mean REALLY like you. I know this guy. He never talked about a girl all last summer. I couldn't even get him to ask me out, and believe me, I tried." She tucked her legs up under her on my bed and looked around as if she were noticing my décor for the first time. "Uh, Laura, I like what you've done with the place. Going for the minimalist look?"

I fell back on bed and laughed at nothing.

Richard was right on time—no surprise—and he immediately focused on Bonnie and then on my Mom and even asked about Dad, who, of course, was under the house looking for the latest leak. Richard gave Mom all the vital statistics she asked for and when Bonnie begged to go with us, he made her think he was actually considering it before Mom intervened.

Decision: Take lessons from Richard.

I WAS surprised that there was nobody else in the car and that we didn't pick anybody else up. It was just the two of us, and he was so nice to me that I almost forgot to act as if I had it all together. It kind of felt like I did.

At the church, he didn't abandon me to a crowd of girls, although he did introduce me to most of them. And later, he made sure we sat together in one of the vans and pulled me into every conversation on the way.

I even held my own, until we got to Hathaway Bridge, which lifted us up over the bay and sailed us down toward the Gulf of Mexico. Then I couldn't talk anymore. The true meaning of the word *breathtaking* made itself apparent, and I plastered my nose to the window.

"You okay?" Richard said. He lowered his voice and let the chatter rise up unnoticed behind us.

"I never saw anything so beautiful in my life," I said.

He looked at me curiously. "This is the first time you've been down here?"

I nodded.

"How long have you lived in P.C., girl?"

"Six weeks."

His face slowly broke into its wonderful metal smile. "Have I got some things to show you, then."

The words sent a delicious chill through me.

And it sure beat the buzz of anxiety.

chapter ten

W hen we pulled into the parking lot at St. Andrew's State
    Park, the youth director—a guy named Ethan who wore an
earring and baggy red shorts and only smiled with his eyes—told
everybody the boundaries. When he turned us loose, kids scattered
everywhere.

Somebody got a volleyball game started.

A couple of other people ran down to the sand with a Frisbee.

Several of the girls, obviously die-hard sunbathers, stripped
down to shorts and bathing suit tops and stretched out on towels
at the water's edge, tanning their goose bumps from what I could
see.

One crew set out for the rocks, which jutted out into the water,
and Richard and I followed that group. Actually, he followed them.
I trailed behind him trying to take it all in.

The Gulf was even more heart-stopping than it had been from
the bridge. As we climbed to the top of one pile of dark gray rocks,

which looked as if some giant child had tumbled them there to play with, I caught my breath and held it.

The Gulf stretched out before me in shades of blue and green, a sea of emeralds sparkling in the sun. The water was so quiet, so soft as it washed up on sand as white and pure as sugar. Just off shore, a pelican sitting atop the water flapped its heavy wings audibly, and then lifted himself into the air. I finally let my breath out in a squeal as he made a pass just above us and landed with an ungraceful plop into the water. His head disappeared and came up, a fish flapping in his beak.

"Oh, my gosh!" I said.

"You ain't seen nothin' yet," Richard said. "This is just the jetty side of the beach."

"I love it!"

I shaded my eyes with my hand as I took in the fishing boats bobbing at the end of the jetty and the large shallow pool formed by the rocks where some children were splashing and digging in delight. Bonnie, I knew, would have loved it there. I could almost hear her laughter on the breeze.

No, that was mine. I was laughing into the wind because there wasn't room in me for anymore beauty. This was too much.

And then Richard grabbed my hand and pulled me from the rocks and up the side of a sand dune to a large gazebo perched on the rise.

"Close your eyes," he said.

"I'll fall on my face!"

"I won't let you," he said.

He took me by the shoulders and put me in front of him. I covered both eyes with my hands and let him guide me to the far side of the gazebo. His hands felt so warm on my arms, I was close to forgetting about the view. Maybe I should have listened to Celeste on the suntan lotion . . .

"Now look," he said.

I uncovered my eyes and stared. Before me was the largest expanse of water I had ever seen, blue-green and dazzling and so clear I could see to the sandy bottom.

"Now that's what I'M talkin' about," Richard said.

"Oh, my gosh," I said again. "That is magnificent." I turned to look at him, nearly colliding my nose into his.

"Can we go down to it?" I said.

"Uh, ya think?"

He grinned at me, braces shimmering in the sun, and took off down the gazebo steps. I raced after him, managing to drag my bag with me and only falling on my face when I got to the sand dune. Then I tumbled ponytail over sandals all the way to the bottom, where Richard, too, was lying in a heap, howling.

"You like to get life all over ya, don'tcha?" he said.

Actually, I'd never thought about myself like that, but since he mentioned it, sure, I could go with that. And I did feel like I wanted to embrace it all, every grain of sand, every droplet of water, every ray of the sun that even in November was baking my face and warming my soul.

I got to my feet and ran for the water with Richard still howling in hot pursuit. I did remember to kick off my Reefers before I plunged in up to my ankles. The cold shock I'd expected didn't happen. The water was just cool and slapped gently against my skin as if it were only teasing me. All I could do was laugh.

Richard laughed with me—for the rest of the afternoon. We walked along the water, wiggling our toes where seagulls left their footprints.

I couldn't decide what I liked best.

The muscular feel of climbing up the sand dunes.

The tiny pieces of broken shells between my toes.

Or Richard.

He asked me questions and listened to my answers. He crawled on the sand on all fours until he found me a whole sand dollar, perfectly intact. And he sat telling me about his life atop a sand dune that sprouted grass like the last few hairs on a bald man's head. It made me think of Mr. Frohm, but that was the only stress-thought I had the whole afternoon and evening.

Decision: This was what it felt like to be in heaven.

They called us for supper, and we sat with six other kids who told me what it was like over at Moseley High and asked me if I knew this person or that person at 'Nama.

"I don't know anybody yet," I told them. "Except Celeste Mancini."

"Oh, you will," said a girl named Anna. "You're so cute, every-body's going to want to know you."

I almost said, *No stinkin' way!* But I remembered to maintain some control.

Besides, I was feeling a little bit cute, the way Richard laughed at me and put ketchup on my nose and ate the remains of the hamburger I just couldn't eat. It wasn't anxiety this time, though. I was just too enthralled with it all to think about food.

"Bonfire in a half-hour," Ethan said. "Have your stuff packed up and ready to go in the van before the fire so we can leave right after."

I, of course, immediately reached for my bag, but Richard shook his head and pulled me to my feet.

"You have to see one more thing," he said.

We left the group behind and climbed out on a jetty, all the way to its point.

"Find yourself a sittin' spot," he said to me.

I located a flat rock that fit my backside perfectly and gave me a place to lean back. Richard settled himself just above me, pointed to the horizon, and said, "Wait."

Then we were quiet. From what seemed like miles away I could hear the other kids hooting and smacking the volleyball. Just below us, the water slapped at the rocks. Beyond, a ship's horn blew as if it were sleepy.

But we were quiet. For the first time since he'd picked me up, the anxiety began to creep back in.

"What are we waiting for?" I whispered.

"Just stay quiet and wait," he whispered back.

I hushed, and told myself I wasn't going to have one of my panic attacks. I was fine. I was happy for a change.

But what if it didn't last?

What if Richard found out I was only pretending to have my life under control?

What if—

And then I saw it. As if it were easing itself into a chair at the end of a long day, the sun sank into the clouds that gathered just over the water. Instantly, the sky turned crimson—and purple—and violet-blue—in strips and streaks and feathers that emblazoned themselves right into my chest. I didn't just see them; I felt them, and the feeling made me cry out.

"Isn't that the best?" Richard whispered to me.

It was. It was because it was too beautiful to be real, and yet it was real. And somehow so was I, in a way I didn't have to try for.

I reached out my arms to the sunset, and Richard gave his pampas grass laugh.

"You can't hold it," he said. "You can only remember it 'til next time."

"But I want it to stay in me!" I said.

Was this God? Was this the passion Mrs. Isaacsen was talking about?

I wanted to ask Richard if he thought it was. I wanted to do something crazy in the sand for God. I wanted God to take me wherever he wanted to.

And then I clamped down on myself. I was losing control and being weird. Richard would think I was some kind of psycho or something. He was so calm about it.

"Let's go, sun worshippers!"

That was Ethan, calling out from the bonfire. His bland voice dissolved the moment.

"You like marshmallows?" Richard said.

"Yeah!"

"Good, because I can't stand them."

He put a hand down and pulled me up. For a second he held it and looked down at me with soft eyes, and then abruptly let go and said, "Race ya!"

He jumped off his rock and took off across the sand, laughing back at me. I picked my way to a jump-off place, and then I turned around to look at the sunset one more time. The last of the purple feathers was fading sadly to gray.

It's just Richard, I thought. *It's just Richard who's making me feel this way.*

Whatever it was, I wanted to keep it.

Next to the fire with Anna and some other kids, Richard was toasting marshmallows for me faster than I could eat them. I had to tell him to stop before I exploded, at which point he shouted, "Let's sing!"

I started to sink.

No singing, please, no singing.

But Ethan miraculously produced a guitar and the circle was suddenly in harmony. The guys across from us stopped the contest they were having to see who could stuff the most marshmallows in their mouth and still say "chubby bunny." It was obviously all about the music with these kids.

"Do you know this one?" Richard whispered to me as they sang, "He's Got the Whole World." Before I could stop myself, I nodded.

"It doesn't matter how bad you are," he said. "We all stink."

I felt a lump forming in my throat. I knew I wasn't going to be able to get even a note out, but I couldn't just sit there like an idiot. I mouthed a few words, and to my own surprise, a melody came out with them. It didn't make me want to cry. In fact, it was as if the song had been waiting for months to be freed, and the joy in its wings as it took flight lifted me up. I was Laura Duffy, and I was singing again.

When "He's Got the Whole World" ended and melted into "Ain't No Rock," Anna grabbed my arm and shook it like I was a Beanie Baby.

"You are so GOOD!" she said. "Did you hear her, Richard?

Richard was smiling at me with his lips closed. His eyes were all sparkly.

"I heard her," he said. "She's awesome. You know 'Lord I Lift Your Name on High'?"

I did. I knew them all, and I sang them all, and I didn't want the music to end.

And it didn't, in a way. We sang in Richard's church the next morning, after I went to Sunday school class with him, and we sang that night at the end of the youth group meeting. On the way home in Richard's car, we even sang with the radio.

He was right; he did kind of stink at singing, but who cared? It was the happiest I had been not just since I'd left Missouri but the happiest ever, in my whole life.

"I just met him!" I told Celeste Monday morning at school. "How can I like him this much?"

"Because it was meant to be," she said. "And because I'm good. Am I good or what?"

I assured her she was the best, because Richard was the best.

And he only got better after that.

I finally had a reason to unpack my computer: For the next three weeks, Richard emailed me every afternoon and called me every night. No more fear of being bummed that no old Missouri friends were writing—it was a thrill to know that there would be a Richard-message waiting for me at every log-on! I was only allowed to talk to him for thirty minutes on the phone, a rule my dad suddenly came up with after the boy came on the scene. That wasn't too bad because then we just got online and instant messaged each other back and forth. Good thing we had a separate phone line for AOL because there was SO much to say.

What's your favorite Bible verse? he asked me one night.

That was easy.

"I waited and waited and waited for God. At last he looked. Finally he listened," I wrote back. *That's from Psalm 40. What's yours?*

"Let the words of my mouth and the meditation of my heart be always acceptable in thy sight," was his answer. *That's what I try to live by.*

Oh, I wrote. *Like your philosophy of life.*

Yeah! So yours is "wait for God?"

I felt a guilty stab. It opened a place for the old anxiety to steal in, and it stung much worse than I remembered it. I put a mental hand on the wound and changed the subject.

Except for that one incident, a mere moment in the grand scheme of things, almost everything was changing for the better.

I was singing with the radio again, mostly love songs. I even practiced a song on the piano to play for Richard if he came over, kind of like a present. It was "Amazing Grace" because I knew he liked that.

I was making A's in all my classes except chemistry, but there was still hope there. Trent, it turned out, was a whiz at tutoring. He'd come into the library looking above my head and muttering stuff. Then as soon as I opened my chemistry book, he started talking like this Harvard professor. But he made it so much clearer than Mr. Frohm did that some things were actually starting to make sense. My grade went up to a B-, and Deidre's went up to a C the minute we became lab partners and I started explaining stuff to HER.

Celeste and I were having a blast, eating lunch together every day and talking on the phone and hanging out with Bonnie and my mom. She was practically starting to LIVE at my house. I even found out I could talk to some of the guys that came to our lunch table without tripping over my tongue. I didn't flirt with them, of course. My heart was reserved for Richard.

Group was good, too. I didn't feel quite so threatened by Joy Beth and K.J. It was like I really did have some control in my life, even the day Mrs. Isaacsen asked us to think about what kept us from acting the way we wanted to act when we were vulnerable.

"I took Michelle's advice," I said. "Now I just act like I know what I'm doing and people believe me."

Michelle gave me an approving nod. Joy Beth didn't. She grunted.

"Could you put that in the form of a question, J.B.?" Mrs. Isaacsen said.

"Okay." Joy Beth honed in on me. "Isn't there a difference between imagining yourself doing something and then doing it, and imagining yourself doing something and just pretending you're doing it?"

"Huh?" Celeste said.

"Do you have an answer for that, Laura?" Mrs. Isaacsen said.

Her eyes were smiling at me. She always gave me confidence.

"I don't think there's that much difference in the end," I said. "I think pretending I have the situation under control makes me feel like I do, and then I do have it under control because I'm more confident."

"Oh, now THAT clears it up—doesn't it?" K.J. said sarcastically.

"I'm not sure it does," Mrs. Isaacsen said.

I looked at her quickly. There was no reassurance in her eyes.

I waited to feel anxious, but I didn't. I just felt a little annoyed. I was being honest like she said to be. What was the deal? I finally felt like I actually had some power in this place, and she was looking at me like I'd just flunked the quiz.

"Do you want to add to that, Laura?" Mrs. Isaacsen said.

I straightened my shoulders. "No," I said. "I think that's pretty much it."

"I don't think I can do that in my situation," Joy Beth said. She was still looking bitterly at me. "I can't pretend my stuff away."

"So what is your stuff?" K.J. said.

"None of your business," Joy Beth snapped back.

"Ladies," Mrs. Isaacsen said softly.

They both retreated to their corners. I could have sworn I saw tears in Joy Beth's eyes, and I felt sorry for her.

Decision: Add her to the youth group prayer list. We prayed together every Wednesday and Saturday nights in small groups. It would feel good to pray for Joy Beth, whatever her "stuff" was.

After our meeting, Mrs. Isaacsen took me aside and asked me if I wanted to come in during study hall.

I could almost hear the tea pouring into the cups. But I could also see the look she'd given me after my answer.

"Um, you know what?" I said. "I've been meaning to tell you this. That last psalm you gave me really worked."

"Oh?" she said. The eyebrows went up. "How so?"

"I waited and waited and waited for God, and he finally listened." I flashed her a smile. "I have a boyfriend!"

For the first time ever, Mrs. Isaacsen looked speechless.

"I know it's like hard to believe," I said.

"Not at all. I just didn't see it coming."

"He's so great. He's even a Christian. I told Celeste I didn't want to meet anybody who wasn't."

"Celeste."

Mrs. Isaacsen looked as if she suddenly understood it all. Her expression nettled at the back of my neck

"She introduced us," I said. "But it isn't like you would think. We go to CHURCH together."

"I love that," Mrs. Isaacsen said. "So let's talk about it more this afternoon. Do you want me to give you a pass now?"

"Well, see, that's just it," I said. "I don't know if I need to come in anymore. I mean, I feel more in control of my life than I ever have, even back in Missouri. I don't even think about moving back anymore. I'm so happy."

Mrs. Isaacsen was nodding her peppery gray head as I talked. "I'm happy for you, Laura," she said. "I am. Just do yourself a favor and don't grasp onto any resolution just to stop you from feeling like you're spinning out of control."

"But I don't think it's like that," I said. I tried not to sound like I did when I was arguing with my mother. "This isn't like making Richard an authority over my life, like you didn't want me to do with you. He's helped me solve my problem, but I'M doing it."

"And I'm glad. Please don't think that I'm not. But there's more to this than your just being homesick then and now you're not. Remember that liminal space, that spiritual place I told you God had led you to?"

"Uh-huh," I said. I could feel some anxiety seeping in. I just wanted to go to lunch with Celeste and laugh and never hear the word *liminal* again.

"You're there for a reason, and it's not so Jesus can come in and solve the problem. What he did, and still does with people, is create spiritual desire in them—make the kind of communion you're searching for with God possible. He teaches us how to BE vulnerable."

"But I don't want to be vulnerable anymore!" said somebody else in me. "I'm sick of that! I want power—you even said I needed power!"

"And I'm trying to teach you how to receive it," she said. "And that's by staying right on the threshold, where you are never in control. You're in a place where you have no choice but to participate in a relationship with God, and that's where your power comes from. Power and control aren't the same things—"

She stopped suddenly. The glow went out of her eyes. "All right," she said. "I certainly don't want you to come in if you don't see a need to. That would be a waste of your time, of course."

She wasn't being sarcastic or bitter, but I felt guilty. And I was as sick of guilty as I was of vulnerable, so I by-passed it to annoyed. I knew she could read it on my face.

"Let me just say two things to you, then," she said. "One, you come in here any time, any time at all. I'm always here for you."

"Okay."

"And two, please make sure you're still taking time to listen to God. That's the key, Laura."

"Right," I said.

I KNEW that. I'd waited to hear from God and he'd sent me Richard and life was good.

"I still want to come to Group, though," I said.

"Yes, please do," she said. "We're starting to gel now. It would hurt everyone if you left."

I didn't know about THAT, but it was nice to hear. On an impulse, I hugged her neck and then skittered out of there, off to Celeste where I could talk about Richard and not feel anything but powerful.

When I was with him, Richard really did give me the feeling that I was on top of everything. I felt that way on Wednesday nights and Sunday nights when we were going to and from Lynn Haven in the car and sitting next to each other at meetings and holding hands in prayer circle. Everybody held hands, but he always made sure we were next to each other when the time came.

That wasn't hard since he pretty much never left my side when we were at church. Other kids like Anna hung with us, but Richard never went off with anybody else. That made me feel special. So did the fact that every Friday night, we did the pizza thing.

We'd never had a pizza night in our family before, but after I went over to Richard's one Friday for HIS family's pie-and-games night, Mom decided we needed to do that, too. I actually preferred going to his house, which I did every other week, because when we were at my house, Bonnie was in his lap the entire time. I got anxious that he was going to get sick of her, but after about five emails on the subject, he told me to please give it up. He loved Bonnie.

I had to admit, I didn't feel AS powerful when I wasn't with Richard, even though the daydreams helped. I was still having trouble going to sleep at night, but usually I could make the anxiety go away if I just wrote him a four-page email, especially if he hadn't called me that evening, or if HIS afternoon email was shorter than two pages.

I typed more than once:

Write me MORE, I want to hear about everything.

He wrote back finally:

My life's not that exciting. LOL.

Of course, I told Celeste every detail. That was half the fun of it. When I told her about that email, she got a wise look on her face. She was doing the English tweed thing that day, and she had her hair up in a loose bun, so it was easy to think she possessed all knowledge at that point.

"What?" I said.

"I think his life could get more exciting," she said.

"How?" I said, slowly dragging out the word.

She leaned across the table toward me and lowered her husky voice. "Has he kissed you yet?"

"No!" I said.

"Not so loud! You'll bring the cops over here." She glanced around as if to make sure we weren't even at that very moment under surveillance. "I didn't think he had."

"I don't think he will," I said. "We talk about that kind of stuff in youth group all the time. I've even heard him say he doesn't believe in having sex before marriage."

"Who said anything about sex? I'm talking about holding hands. Putting your arms around each other. Kissing each other on the lips—"

"Okay, stop," I said.

I had both hands to my cheeks to make sure they weren't on fire. Celeste laughed out loud.

"You are SO innocent!" she said.

"It's not my fault! I've never been this close to a guy before. And it's about as close as I'm going to get. Richard doesn't act like he wants to—do all that stuff."

"That's because he thinks you don't want to do it." She looked at me over the tops of the clear-lens glasses she was wearing. "You do, don't you?"

I looked down at the tabletop. "I don't know," I said.

"Trust me, you do," Celeste said. "Once he holds you one time, you're going to turn into a total cuddler, I can see it. And I'm not talkin' sex. I'm just talkin'—nice."

I found myself staring at her. The English ensemble didn't disguise the look on her face. She could have been wearing a monkey suit and I still would have seen it. There was a deep long-ing in her eyes, a wistfulness that was unmistakably sad.

"Anyway!" she said brightly. "I wouldn't give you this advice if you were going out with the average guy."

"Why not?" I said.

"Because the average guy wants to go straight from cuddling right into the sack. Then you have to constantly fight him off or dump him."

"But I don't want to dump Richard!"

"You won't have to because he isn't the average guy. He has these standards that go like, way deep. I don't get it, but it's true. I know the reason he wouldn't go out with me was because he was afraid I was going to try to get HIM into bed. But see, with you, it would be very slow, very innocent."

"But what if he really doesn't want to?"

Celeste looked suddenly maternal. "Of course he does. He's male. He's just a male in control of himself. You have no idea how lucky you are. The thing is, your relationship has gone on long enough that it has to go to the next level."

"How many levels are there?" I said. Reruns of *Friends* flashed through my mind.

"Don't worry about it," she said. "By the time you get to THAT level, you'll be ready to get married."

"Married!" I said.

Half the courtyard turned around and stared. "Oh no, the "M" word!" one guy yelled out. "Run for your lives!"

"I told you to hold it down," Celeste hissed at me.

"You've got us married already?"

"You don't see this as a forever relationship?" Celeste said.

"I don't know."

"I do. I think you two could be so good together. But you've got to keep it interesting."

"I kiss HIM? No stinkin' way!"

"No, you don't kiss him first, but you may have to make a move in that direction. Let him know it's okay."

"And I do that how?" I said. My face was still bright red, I could feel it, but I was starting to get interested in an embarrassed, awkward kind of way. Bless Celeste; she could talk to me about this stuff without making me feel like a TOTAL idiot.

"When are you guys alone?" she said.

"Never. Well, when we're in the car going to and from church."

"Okay. When you're in the car, let some silences fall, especially when you're stopped at a red light or something. Look at him like you really, REALLY like him. And don't be afraid to touch him, you know, just like in passing. Brush your hand against his or something."

I was already breaking out into a sweat and Richard wasn't even in the same building. Celeste took one look at me and laughed out loud.

"SHHH!" I said to her. "YOU'll bring the cops!"

"Too late," she said. She nodded over her shoulder. I glanced back to see Mr. Stennis coming toward us.

"Were we making that much noise?" I said.

My sweat was turning to ice.

"How ya'll doin?" Mr. Stennis said behind me.

"Good," Celeste said. "You wanna sit down? Have a cookie?"

She offered him an Oreo, but he shook his head and turned to me.

"I just thought you'd want to know that they finally put Shayla Cunningham in the juvenile detention facility. Three months minimum. You don't have to worry 'bout her doggin' your trail anymore."

I didn't have to fake the smile I gave him.

"I knew you'd like that news," he said. "And you go on and be proud of yourself. You had a lot to do with putting her there."

He patted me on the shoulder, nodded at Celeste, and left to scope out the rest of the courtyard. At the table beside us, a guy took his cigarettes out of his shirt pocket and stuffed them into his backpack.

"You rock," Celeste said to me when Mr. Stennis was out of earshot. "You totally rock."

"Whatever," I said.

Between daydreaming about possibly, maybe, kissing Richard, and thinking about making the school safe from Shayla, my little chest was just puffing out and my head was floating about six inches above my shoulders. I was smiling at everybody on my way to my locker after school.

Until I got there and saw something so strange, it drained my veins.

chapter eleven

"What the HECK?" I said out loud.

That attracted the attention of a guy three lockers away, who looked down at mine and said, "Dude, you got somethin' growin' on your locker."

No kidding. I squatted down and stared at a bare stick-like thing that appeared to have sprouted out of the metal and had attached itself diagonally across my locker door. But it wasn't just a random twig. There were tiny bulges sprouting along its bareness that promised to become buds.

I sat on my heels and disentangled myself from my backpack, never taking my eyes off of the plant. I don't know what I expected—for it to open one of its little buds and speak to me like—something out of *Little Shop of Horrors*? For it to start sprouting leaves? I didn't know. I just knew that I expected something. It wasn't a conscious thought; it was a sensation, a warmth, and a pull that made me want to touch it.

Just as I stretched my fingers slowly toward it, a voice broke into the moment.

"Hey, Laura, could you—what is THAT?"

It was Deidre.

She joined me in a squat, tossing back her red hair and squinting through her glasses.

"Okay," she said. She had a tiny mouth and a tiny bud-like smile, which she now directed at me. "Your boyfriend has a weird sense of what's romantic. I'd rather have a rose myself."

"It's not from my boyfriend. He doesn't even go here."

"So who put the grape vine on your locker?"

"Is that what it is?" I said.

"Yeah. My mother makes wreaths out of them. This is an INTERESTING look anyway." She tilted her head at me. "But, then, you're an interesting person."

I didn't answer. This was all so strange.

"I don't mean that in a bad way," Deidre said.

"Huh?" I said.

"When I said you were interesting, I didn't mean like weird or strange. I just meant you're cool, only not in the usual way."

I peeled my eyes from the vine to look at her. My face must have looked as befuddled as hers was, because she laughed, a shriek of a laugh, like a surprised goose. A laugh bubbled up out of me too.

"Do you WANT that on your locker?" Deidre said. "I mean, if you don't, my mother would do something with it. She thinks she's Martha Stewart."

I wasn't sure I wanted to give the vine away, for some reason. It was as if it were trying to say something to me . . .

Okay, wow. I was going beyond *interesting*. Plants speaking to me? That was more like *psycho*.

"Sure, she can have it," I said. "It's kind of weirding me out."

Still, I gingerly took hold of it with my fingers and gave it only a gentle tug. It didn't come loose. It was as if it were clinging to the locker for its little life.

"How's it attached?" Deidre said.

"I don't know. It's like it's grown into the metal."

"Okay, now THAT is weird."

Which was exactly what I was afraid of. I pulled harder on the vine. *Come on, thing, before they start calling me the school mental case.*

"That is ON there," Deidre said. "I think it's attached from the inside. Open your locker and let's see."

An unfamiliar sensation, a pressure, eased into my chest. I didn't know whether to be afraid of it or not. I did know that I didn't want to open my locker. Visions of roots digging down into the pages of my history book were taking shape in my head.

"I don't have time," I said, standing up. "I have to go pick up my little sister."

"You, too? I've got brother duty three days a week. I have no life anymore." Deidre smiled her rosebud of a smile. "So, can I call you tonight and get help with the chem homework?"

"Sure," I said.

So, she was suddenly being nice to me because she needed my help? My heart sank a little as I rattled off my phone number.

It probably would have sunk further if I hadn't still been preoccupied with this vine thing. I waited until Deidre was gone and there were only a few students rattling around in the hallway before I put my hand up to the plant again. It was real. It was a living thing—I could practically feel the life pulsating through it: chlorophyll or nitrogen or whatever it was that coursed through the veins of plants. It was crazy, and yet it was as if my senses were suddenly heightened. The tips of my fingers were warming. I could smell the freshness of the swollen places soon to burst into leaf—

Okay, wow. Enough. I reached for the combination lock and spun the dial.

Don't be an idiot, I told myself. *This is just somebody's idea of a joke. And there's nothing in here. How's somebody going to get inside my locker? I heard they have to get a court order before they can even search the thing for drugs.*

Still, my heart was beating like a piston as I gave the lock its final twirl and lifted the handle. I swung the door open to find nothing. Nothing but my stack of textbooks, binders, and folders, which I lunged at with great gusto. As I coaxed my chemistry book from the bottom of the pile, a piece of white folded paper fell out onto the floor.

I stopped, my chem book only halfway out, precariously unbalancing the whole stack. The piece of paper, a heavy expensive-looking vellum, lay at my feet like an intruder I'd discovered invading my familiar world.

I shoved the books back into the locker, still staring at it.

Okay, come on, Laura. Stop psyching yourself out. Somebody pushed it through the crack. Probably Celeste. Who else is going to be writing you a note around here?

I stooped down, hand outstretched to pick it up, when the answer to that question made me snatch my fingers back.

Shayla. Some messenger of hers had stuck it in there.

What if it was a threat? What if Shayla had marshaled some of her cigarette-smoking friends against me from inside the pen? What if Keesha had heard about Shayla's incarceration and was determined not to end up the same way because of my testimony?

You are going to drive yourself batty! I thought. *Just pick it up and read it. Have some power over your life for once!*

I snatched up the paper and nearly ripped it as I unfolded it. The words inside were penned in perfect calligraphy. That eliminated Shayla right off the bat.

> *Please listen to me. I want you to know me.*
> *A Secret Admirer.*

I nearly melted into a puddle of relief. It wasn't Shayla. It wasn't Keesha. It wasn't anybody I needed to be afraid of.

"What I KNOW," I said out loud, "is that you're a freak." I laughed weakly and tucked the note into my backpack. *Somebody is just weird,* I thought. I was almost giddy as I collected the books I needed for homework and slammed the door. "Sorry," I said to the vine, "but I already have a boyfriend."

I definitely needed to remove the plant life. There was some kind of rule about not putting anything on the outside of your locker. But I was already about to miss the bus, and I had to pick up Bonnie. For the moment, I put Mr. Secret Admirer out of my mind.

But it kept coming back to me all afternoon. I got out the Candy Land game and tried to focus on getting to the ice cream sandwich before Bonnie did. But I couldn't get the vine, the note, or the Secret Admirer out of my mind. I couldn't ignore the way I'd felt when I'd been close to the vine, as if I could feel it living.

"What do?"

I looked up from the game board at Bonnie.

"Huh?" I said.

"It's your turn. How come you don't go?"

"Because I was going to give you an extra turn," I said.

"How come?"

"Because you're too cute," I said.

She shook the curls that begged to be tugged. "That's not why. You were thinking 'bout Richard. You love him."

A laugh burst out of me. I sounded like Deidre. "Love?" I said. "You're watching too much TV."

"Are you gonna marry him?"

"No!"

Her eyes clouded over. "Why not?"

"Because we're sixteen. Hello!"

"But when you're bigger, will you?" Her face puckered in concern. "Will I be too old to be a flower girl?"

"You'll have a cane and dentures before anybody marries me!" I said. "Are you going to take your extra turn, or are you going to let me beat you?"

Bonnie went gleefully back to the land of candy, and my mind drifted away again.

Somebody did admire me, even if he WAS kind of a freak about it. I had to admit that was a little cool. It made me feel—well—powerful.

Okay, God, I thought, unexpectedly. *So you did listen.*

Maybe I was finally off that threshold Mrs. Isaacsen kept talking about.

The phone jangled me out of my reverie and I dove for it before Bonnie could get it. It was Celeste.

"Get another game," I whispered to Bonnie. "Get Chutes and Ladders. I can beat you at that."

"Can't," she said, and bounced off.

When she was out of earshot, I told Celeste about the "Secret Admirer."

"Get outa town!" she said. "And you don't have any idea who it is? You haven't noticed anybody, like, checking you out?"

"No!" I said.

"That's the beauty of it." Celeste's voice was going into intense mode. She was getting into it.

"What's that mean?" I said.

"There's nothing better for the female ego than somebody checkin' you out from afar. And you can so use this to your advantage."

"Like how?"

"Hello? Richard."

"What about him?"

I could feel her giving me a blank stare. "I love you, Laura," she said. "But sometimes you are so clueless. Remember we talked about getting some excitement into your relationship? This could do that so fast."

"You mean tell HIM about this?"

"Uh, ya think? Let him know there's a little competition and that first kiss is a done deal."

"Like make him jealous?"

"No. I hate that game. Just make him aware that you are attractive to other guys and that if he wants to hold onto you, he'd better stake his claim."

"What?!"

Celeste gave her husky chuckle. "Okay, so wrong words, but you get my drift. It adds a little mystery to the relationship, you know what I'm sayin'?"

"I guess so," I said. "I'm so bad at this."

"You're not bad. You're just inexperienced." The eyebrow wiggling came clearly through the phone line. "That's why you got me."

But after we hung up, I couldn't decide whether to tell Richard or not. It seemed kind of mean, somehow. I'd hate it if he told me some girl was leaving him notes and grape vines. Hate it? I'd go straight into one of those anxiety things.

Besides, there was something about that vine, the way it wouldn't let go, the way it was still alive on that cold piece of metal, that made it seem as if it were attached to me. And only me.

You ARE a nut case! I told myself firmly. *Forget the whole Secret Admirer thing and concentrate on Richard. You have to make this relationship more exciting for him.*

After Mom got home, I went to my room and practiced a soft voice I could use when Richard called. That, too, seemed crazy, but THAT I could chalk up to having Richard Fever. It was a crazy I could go with.

But it was a waste of time because Richard didn't call me that night, and there was no email from him. I would have killed to have been able to pick up the phone and call him, but that was so taboo with Mom and Dad. Having a boy in my life had definitely magnified the rule situation in our house.

By the time I read Bonnie about eight books, walked Deidre through the chemistry assignment on the phone, and did the rest of my own homework, I was feeling the buzz in my veins.

There had been times when Richard had been late calling me or couldn't call me or only wrote me a short email. But this felt different. It was ME—I didn't know what to do with my thoughts because I wasn't talking to him, and I wasn't sure he was thinking about me. Doubts crept in like smoke under a door.

I checked the phone to make sure it was working.

I checked my email so many times I was hearing "You've Got Mail" over and over in my head. The only messages were from Celeste and people wanting to sell me prescription drugs.

I ignored both of them and went straight to "Write." I suddenly felt desperate, as if my plane were about to crash. Sweaty palms. Dry mouth. Dread in the pit of my stomach. Forget getting Richard to kiss me. I just wanted to HEAR from him. I had to know if he still—well, if he just—still.

Dear Richard.

Delete. Too formal.

Rich—

Delete. Too casual. Besides, I never called him Rich.

Hi, Richard.

That would work. A tiny voice whispered, *Write "Hello, my Richard-friend."* But that sounded too cutesy. I had serious things to say in this email.

> *I didn't hear from you all day and I'm worried about you. Actually, I'm a little freaked out. Are you okay? Usually you call or email or both (my personal favorite!) and when you didn't, I started imagining all kinds of things. Were you in a car accident? Did someone break your leg at basketball practice? Were you trapped under something heavy? Abducted by aliens?*

I deleted that last one. It just kind of bubbled out of me, but it seemed too light for what I was leading up to.
What AM I leading up to? I thought. *Get to the point, Laura.*
I wrote:

> *Anyway, if any of those things happened to you, you're probably not read-ing this email. I hope somebody calls me so I can be there for you.*
> *If you're actually okay, then I'm REALLY worried. I'm so used to hearing from you and talking to you about things. I can always talk to you, you know? It's like you're this important part of my life now, and I want that to go on and on.*

Was that okay? Was I coming on too strong?
I left it. I could always go back and delete it before I sent it. Besides, the whole thing was taking on a life of its own. Maybe that was my power. Maybe the power was in being completely honest.

> *I'm telling you all this because I want you to know how important it is to me that you write me and call me. It's like I have to see you and talk to you or I'm not okay. You've given me so much—you don't even know—and you're like some kind of lifeline or something. I'm under a lot of pressure to get good grades and I've told you how I felt like I got ripped out of my whole life when I had to move here. But all I have to do is hear your voice and I'm good to go again. It's like you've given me a life here and I love that!*
> *So, see, I have to talk to you every day and get emails and be around you. I don't know what else that means, but whatever it is, I'm there.*

I sat back and studied that for a second. It seemed kind of out there. But it was what I felt. And Celeste would have said to go for it, I was sure of that. Geez, she was ready for me to marry the guy. She AND Bonnie.

I closed my eyes, just for a second, to envision walking down the aisle in a pristine white dress with pearls encrusting the train, smiling through my filmy veil at Richard, whose own smile was misted with tears of total happiness.

If you can envision it, Joy Beth had said, *you can make it happen.* Or something like that.

Could I make this happen? Did I have that kind of power?

Or not?

What if not? What if Richard was just losing interest in me, period? What if I were suddenly dumped and left right back in the middle of the dead end I'd started on before I met him?

I was suddenly cold and sweaty. Dread came down on me as if losing Richard had already happened.

I fumbled my shaking fingers back to the keyboard and typed hard and fast.

> *Just call me, all right? I just need to hear your voice and I'll be okay. You are the best. You are MY best—*

"Laura. Are you still online?"

I jumped. My fingers leapt to the mouse and clicked on the SEND icon. The message disappeared off into cyberspace just as my father flicked on the light and came to stand behind my chair.

"I'm just getting off," I said. The mouse was scurrying to CLOSE and EXIT and SIGN OFF NOW and every other key I could find to cover my tracks. I suddenly felt guilty, sneaky, and wrong.

"I need to get on this computer," Dad said. "Mine's down."

"Sure," I said.

If I hadn't been in mental turmoil at that point, I might have taken more notice of the fact that this was the first conversation I'd had alone with my father since the day Bonnie was in the hospital, weeks ago. I did check out the fact that he was looking grayer and thinner, and somehow taller as a result. His eyes, wide and brown like mine, were pinched at the corners, and there were lines there that couldn't have been there two weeks ago. My father was getting old.

"You tired, Dad?" I said.

"What?" he said. He was looking at the chair I was getting out of.

"Are you tired? You look tired."

"It's eleven o'clock at night," he said. "Yeah, I'm tired."

My heart did that sinking thing. I wasn't sure why. My father and I hadn't exactly been bosom buddies the last eight months.

Why should I expect anything else out of him except the implication that I really did ask the stupidest questions?

"Good night," I said.

He didn't answer until I was past the fish tank and almost out the family room door.

"Laura," he said.

"Yes, sir?" I said.

"Thanks for asking," he said.

We exchanged a look before he turned abruptly to the computer screen. It was a look that begged for more, but didn't know how to get it.

There was so much to think about, to stress over, when I climbed into bed that I immediately turned on the TV. No radio music tonight. I was afraid of it again.

And afraid that Richard would never answer my email.

And afraid that my father was growing into an old man.

And afraid that the power I'd started to feel was going to drift away.

My anxiety was just a muddle of nothingness when I got to school the next morning. However, I was jolted into reality in short order when I arrived at my locker.

One of the maintenance crew was there with a pair of hand clippers, hacking away at my vine. I wanted to shout, "Stop! You'll hurt it!"

"This your locker?" he said as my shadow fell over him.

"Yes, sir," I said.

He looked up and scowled at me from under eyebrows as thick as a hedge. "I don't know how you got this on here, but I'm having a time gettin' it off."

"I didn't put it on there," I said, my heart starting to race. Visions of Mr. Stennis's office were already dancing in my head.

"Then tell your prankin' friends not to deface school property. Happens again, I'll hafta report it."

There was no use trying to explain to the janitor that somebody I didn't even KNOW had left me this strange little gift. And even though I wanted to, I knew it was pointless to tell him to be gentle with it, or at least let me be the one to take it off. I just muttered, "Yes, sir," and decided not to bother with my books for first period. I could wing it through English.

Somehow, the fact that even Mr. Clean couldn't get the vine loose gave the whole thing an even deeper dimension. I felt like there was somebody following me, and yet it wasn't a sinister presence. It was just as if there were somebody there, somebody who could do things that out-janitored the janitor.

Now that it was daylight and I had Celeste and her stable of men and funny Deidre in chemistry class and Trent enlightening me on aluminum chlorhydrate, I felt the dread lifting. I actually got quiet during study hall, since everybody else was napping, and thanked God for listening. It was a good time to remind myself that it was Wednesday and that I would see Richard tonight. It WAS going to be okay.

I raced home with Bonnie that afternoon and for the first time since her allergy attack plugged her into a *Veggie Tales* video and went for the computer. I had mail, and my first message was from Richard. I clicked onto Read with a giggle in my throat.

He'd written:

> *Laura,*
> *I'll pick you up tonight at the regular time, okay?*
> *You're important to me too. We'll talk.*
> *Richard*

At the bottom was his favorite Bible verse.

> *"May the words of my mouth and the meditations of my heart be always acceptable in thy sight."*

Had that always been there? If it had, I'd never noticed, but I decided to answer in kind.

I wrote back:

> *Richard,*
> *Can't wait.*
> *Laura*
> *"I waited and waited and waited for God.*
> *At last he looked; finally he listened."*

I added:

> *And then he gave me you.*

"Did you get an email from Richard?" Bonnie asked when I joined her on the couch just in time to see David the asparagus clobber the giant pickle right between the eyes while peas and olives looked on.

"I did," I said happily. "I'm important to him."

"He loves you," Bonnie said.

"Maybe he does," I said. "Just maybe he does."

chapter twelve

A nd then again, maybe he didn't.
   I couldn't tell when Richard came to pick me up that night.
   He was as nice as ever to my mom, and of course, he threw
Bonnie up on his shoulder and made her shriek to be put down
and then shriek to do the whole thing over again.
   But when we got in his car, and I said, "So, how are ya?" he just
said, "I'm good." And that was it.
   There was a long silence, during which I couldn't think of
anything to say except, *What's the MATTER? Do you hate me? You
hate me, don't you?* (Which at least I had enough sense not to say.)
   He turned on the radio, and I pretended to be getting into Jars of
Clay, but I was actually trying to get my mind to stop clawing at
the walls of my skull.
   For Pete's sake, Laura, you're freaking out! I told myself. *You said a
bunch of stuff to him last night. He probably doesn't even know where to
start. Give the guy a break.*

And look at him like you really, really like him.

That last part came from Celeste, of course, but this seemed like as good a time as any to give it a try.

I had to do SOMETHING.

Unfortunately, the look I delivered just as he glanced over, probably to find out just what the heck I was staring at, was somewhere between simpering desperation and rising nausea. I topped it off with a nice inane giggle.

"You okay?" he said.

Yes! He spoke! He cared!

"Oh, yeah," I said. "I'm good. Are we going to talk?"

"We can talk. Go for it."

"No," I said, forcing a laugh. "I mean, I can definitely do that, big surprise. I'm talking about your email. You said WE'D talk."

"Oh, yeah," he said. In the flash of oncoming headlights, I saw the two little pink spots appear in his cheeks. "Can we do that later?"

"'Course," I said.

I was touched by his sudden nervousness. Or was I just so nervous myself I couldn't imagine anyone being anything else? In fact, I don't even know if it was desperation or Celeste hissing in my ear, *Do it! Just do it!* that made me reach over and put my hand over his on the gearshift. I gave it a squeeze that was meant to communicate, *It's okay. This is way different for me too.*

Whether he got that message or not, I had no idea. The second I pulled my hand away, he plastered his to the steering wheel and didn't move it until we got to the church, except to turn up the radio so talking was impossible. My heart took a nosedive I couldn't pull it out of.

In fact, everything went into a dive after that.

As soon as we crossed the threshold into the youth room, Anna was suddenly at my elbow, asking me a stream of questions she really didn't give me a chance to answer about where I bought my shoes and how I got my hair into a French braid by myself and whether I ever listened to NPR. Between sputtered attempts at replies, I twisted my head around to look for Richard, but he was nowhere to be found.

When we sat down for Ethan's opening spiel, I was elbowed between Anna and her best friend Jen. Richard was across the room with a pack of guys who had him in stitches. Guys I'd never even seen him talk to before.

Whatever Ethan said bounced right off of me. My mind was too stuffed with fear to let anything else in. When we got up to do some activity where we were supposed to move magnets around on a map to find True North, I shoved my chair around aimlessly, all the while craning my neck to see Richard. He was focused on the task at hand. Then he was punching some jock on the biceps. Then he was doing everything except acknowledging the fact that I was continually begging him with my eyes.

When we got to the chips and dips, a girl named Christina came up to me, eyes all sympathetic, and said, "Did you and Richard break up?" Anna stuffed a handful of Doritos into her mouth and Jen said to me, "Cute shoes, Duffy. Where did you get them?"

Suddenly the room reeked of conspiracy. I left Jen still saying, "Payless? Did you get them at Payless?" and dodged around a circle of boys guzzling Mountain Dew to get to Richard. He was deep in conversation with Ethan, so I just stood there, expectantly, until they both looked up at me.

"How you doin', Laura?" Ethan said.

"I'm fine. I just need to talk to Richard."

Ethan cocked an eyebrow at Richard that said it all. He, too, knew why Richard was avoiding me like I had hepatitis C. He even punctuated it with a pat on Richard's shoulder before he slipped away.

"What's going on?" I said.

"Why?" Richard said. He put his Coke can to his lips and chugged it.

"Well, I mean, usually you sit with me and stuff." I knew I sounded pathetic and I hated it. I tried to smile and added, "Did I forget to put on deodorant?"

"No! You smell fine!"

Okay, so he was floundering, too. I clung to that as a good sign.

"I just thought maybe you oughta get to know some of the other kids in here," he said. "You know, Anna and them."

"O-oh," I said. "So that's what Ethan was telling you."

He just looked at me.

"I'm perfectly content just hanging out with you," I said. I slipped into the soft voice I'd been practicing for just this moment. "I come here because I want to be with you."

"Hey! Are ya'll coming to worship?"

It was Anna behind me, hands on my shoulders, talking in a too-cheery voice. I wanted to wrench away from her and tell her, tell them ALL, that I could handle my own affairs, thank you very much. Instead, I just held my breath and waited for Richard to answer. When he did, my heart made its final crash landing.

"Y'all go ahead," he said. "I'll be there in a minute."

In one last, desperate, pitiful attempt to salvage hope, I saved him a seat in the church. He never showed, at least not next to me. When it was over and I turned around, he was three rows behind us, sitting with Ethan and still avoiding eye contact with me. I couldn't wait to get into the car, because I was going to get to the bottom of this if I had to pluck it out of him with tweezers.

Except that when I met him in the parking lot, Anna and Jen were in the back seat.

"We begged a ride," Anna said to me in that same too-happy voice that had been climbing up the cheerful scale all evening. Jen just giggled.

And then the three of them chattered non-stop all the way up 231, with Richard making up for not uttering a word in the car earlier. We were all the way to the Lynn Haven-Panama City line before I realized that Richard was taking me home first. At that point, I could hardly fight back the tears.

When he pulled into my driveway, I ignored Anna and Jen's invitations to "email me, girl!" and bolted out of the car. Richard made a half-hearted attempt to walk me to the door, and stood on the bottom step of our front porch, looking up at me. Sort of. His eyes darted from mine to the door to the porch light to everywhere but back to me.

"Call me when you get home," I said. "I have to talk to you."

He didn't say he would. And he didn't.

When it got past ten o'clock, I flung myself on my bed and cried for a long time—hard, painful sobs that threatened to rip my ribs apart. When I couldn't cry anymore, I reached for the remote, but I couldn't click it on. The "Friends" would be talking about nothing but guys, relationships, the Richards of the world who built you up and then let you down.

But without sounds, the panic crashed in and there was nothing I could do to stop it. I just lay there, listening to it buzz in my head, through my veins, up and down every nerve passage until I was breathing so hard I had to sit up or I knew, I just knew, I would die.

Get quiet and listen, Mrs. Isaacsen had said. Wonderful. All I was hearing was the future proclaiming its doom to me: *If he really dumps you, if Richard really doesn't want a relationship anymore, then you're back to being New Girl, Nobody. You blew it, and your power is gone.*

Decision: "It's going to work out," I said—out loud, so I would believe it. "I have to make it work out, because I can't stand to lose

Richard. I can't stand it."

But there was nothing in that determination but words, and they were swallowed up by the darkness. Then there was only the buzz. I tried to whisper over it: "Why does this happen to me, God? Why do I try so hard and it just isn't working out—ever?"

After that, I cried myself into a sleep that left me exhausted.

I missed the bus the next morning, and Mom was NOT happy about having to drive me to school. That was okay. At least she was so wrapped up in being annoyed she didn't seem to notice that I was toting several large pieces of luggage under my eyes.

By the time I got to the lockers everybody and their mother seemed to be there, milling in a stalled, agitated mob. I tried to move through it, but I was met with elbows in the nose and shoulders under the chin and one particularly hard jab right in the solar plexus.

"What's going on?" I shouted over the din, to no one in particular.

Nobody answered me except a tall, slender guy beside me who had a ponytail halfway down his back.

"There's been another fight," he said.

Must be a bad one, I thought. The guy didn't sound bloodthirsty the way kids usually did when there was a smackdown going on in the hall. Since my confrontations with Shayla and Keesha, I'd learned that there were at least two fights a week at 'Nama Beach, and that was when things were slow.

I turned to try to work my way out of the crowd, but there was no way. They were like the Berlin Wall behind me, and THIS one wasn't coming down. A rise in the crowd's general state of anticipation turned me around again, and I had to grab onto somebody's sleeve so I wouldn't be knocked down by everyone parting the waters to let Mr. Stennis and the SRO through. Between them was a hulking dark-haired boy with blood smeared across his face.

It was Trent.

My gasp could be heard above the mob.

"You know Trent?" Ponytail Boy said.

"He's my chemistry tutor!"

"Dude, what a dork, huh?"

That came from another guy with a sad attempt at a goatee who seemed to find the whole thing amusing. I turned to register my disgust with the only other sympathetic person present—Ponytail Boy—but he was gone. By then, Stennis and Mr. SRO had already passed by me. They were half-carrying Trent, and I could only see him from behind, his bloody head hanging down over hunched shoulders as if he could hardly stand the shame.

"I know your pain," I whispered.

I couldn't wait to get to Group that day, and when Mrs. Isaacsen asked if anybody had anything they wanted to share before we got started, my hand was up.

"Did you guys see that fight this morning?" I said. "Did anybody see what happened?"

"It was two metal heads," K.J. said. "They jumped this math geek, like, for no reason. He was big—I mean, the guy is huge—but he just stood there like a digit-head and let them wale on him."

"He's not just a digit-head," I said. "He's my chemistry tutor, and he's the sweetest guy. I know he doesn't fit in and have all this popularity and stuff, but he doesn't deserve to get beat up on. I hate that. I'm sick of it! I'm sick of people who are just trying to live their lives getting kicked in the teeth because they're not this or they're not that—"

I only stopped then because I had to take a breath. There was so much more in me that was suddenly there, screaming to get out.

"Well, who'd a thought?" Joy Beth said.

"Thought what?" Mrs. Isaacsen said.

"She's human. Laura."

"What did you think she was, a mannequin?" K.J. said.

"I just didn't think she ever got mad, is all. And then, boom, she's like a nuclear explosion."

"I'm not done exploding," I said. "'Cause you know what, I'm not gonna be this wimp anymore. I'm going to take some control."

"How you plan to do that?" Joy Beth said.

I looked at her and felt my face collapsing. "I have no idea," I said. I looked at Michelle, who handed me her packet of Kleenex.

"I know one thing," Mrs. Isaacsen said. "Sheer muscle and will power aren't going to make it happen."

"Then what does?" Michelle said.

She—all of us—were leaning forward, waiting with our empty plates for Mrs. Isaacsen to fill them.

But for the first time since I'd known her, Mrs. Isaacsen looked helpless, as if she couldn't find the words to give us.

"Don't you know?" K.J. said. "What the HECK, dude!"

"I know," Mrs. Isaacsen said. "But I can't share that with you, a captive audience in a public school. It has to do with my faith."

"So don't say it like it's fact," K.J. said. "Just tell us what YOU believe. Then we can do whatever we want with it."

Mrs. Isaacsen looked around the room. "Is that all right with everyone?"

We all nodded, all but Celeste. She didn't even look like she was listening. When Mrs. Isaacsen said, "Okay, Celeste?" she nodded vacantly, and I knew she had absolutely no idea what she was agreeing to.

"All right," Mrs. Isaacsen said. "I believe that only the Holy Spirit can give the kind of power Laura is talking about."

"And we're going to get that how?" Michelle said.

"It's a gift from God. We only have to say yes to it."

"So where is it?" K.J. said. She was looking around the office as if she expected it to pop out of one of the file cabinets.

"It's in every word Jesus speaks. Every word of his is life making. That's what I believe."

There was a silence in the room I could have reached out and touched. I could have gathered it up in my arms. Across it, Mrs. Isaacsen looked at me, and into me. I wanted to throw myself into her arms and say, "Help me! Please, help me!"

When Group was over, I hung back to ask her if I could come see her today, but Celeste tugged at my arm. It was the first time she'd really even looked at me all period.

"Let's hurry up and go to lunch," she said. "I gotta talk to you."

An idea suddenly kicked over in my head, revving up its little engine.

"Can we go to the mall for lunch today?" I said as I hurried down the hall after her. "Do you have your car? I'll buy you food."

Celeste stopped and frowned at me. "Why do you want to go to the mall?" she said. "You know I hate that."

I looked at the floor. "I was kind of hoping Richard would be there and I could talk to him. I think we have—some issues."

"Come on," she said. "You and I definitely gotta talk."

We went to our in-the-corner table, and Celeste sat with her back resolutely to the male world. Neither one of us opened our lunches.

"What?" I said. "You want to say something—WHAT?"

She pressed her lips together before she spoke. I noticed, oddly, that she was just wearing jeans and a T-shirt. No fashion statement today.

"Celeste, is everything okay?" I said. "I mean, is it your dad? Did you hear from your mom or something?" I grabbed her hand and held it between my clammy palms. "I'm sorry. I was so all-about-Richard I wasn't even thinking. I'm such a selfish idiot sometimes. Come on, what's wrong?"

She was just looking at me, her eyes big and sad, waiting in some kind of agony for me to take a breath.

"It's not about me," she said "It's about you."

"Me?" I said.

"Laur', I think you oughta start playing the field."

"WHAT?"

"This whole relationship thing—"

"But you said that was what I needed!"

"I was wrong, all right? And I feel like a moron. But I think, after lookin' at it, that you maybe ought to date around some before you settle into a relationship. Stay single for a while."

I could feel my heart heading for a thud again. "Did you talk to Richard?" I said.

"This is comin' from here," she said, hand to her chest.

"Celeste?"

She sighed and muttered something under her breath, which, I was sure, was a cuss word.

"He called me last night after church," she said "Only I promised I wouldn't tell you."

"Why? What did he say?"

"What am I, talking to myself here? I told him I wouldn't tell you!"

"Then why did you bring this whole thing up?"

"Because I didn't want you to feel like you were hit by a bus when he talks to you!"

"Then he is going to talk to me? When?"

"When he gets up the guts, I guess."

She took a sudden interest in unzipping her lunch box. I grabbed her by the wrist. "What's he going to say to me?" I said.

"I'm not telling you anymore."

Then Celeste set her jaw stubbornly, and I knew the conversation was over. It was so over that I excused myself from the table and spent the rest of lunch in the girls' restroom, waiting for the dizziness to drive me into a stall to throw up. It never did, but I barely got through the remainder of the day. I joined the comatose state that fell over most of study hall and then asked for a pass to see the nurse during my last two classes so I could curl up into a fetal position on a cot, feigning cramps, until the bell rang. All I wanted to do was stay numb until I could talk to Richard. If I did anything else, I was afraid I'd go into an anxiety hole I'd never pull out of.

The minute Bonnie and I got home, I sat her next to a stack of videos with one in the VCR and turned up the volume. I was on my way to the kitchen when she muted it and said, "Are you mad at me, Laurie?"

I could feel the tears gathering like a flash flood.

"No, Baby!" I said. "What makes you think I'm mad at you?"

"Because you're not playin' with me."

I had to put my hand over my mouth to keep from sobbing right out loud. I went over to her and pulled her into my lap so she couldn't see my face.

"I'm going to play with you," I said. "There is nothing I would rather do in the whole world than play with you. I just have to take care of something first."

"You're crying," she said.

She tried to twist around on my lap, but I couldn't let her. I knew there was pain etched on my face that her pure, little girl eyes shouldn't see. She'd never understand it.

"I'm not crying," I said. "I've got something stuck in my throat. Let me go do my thing and I'll be back and we'll play whatever you want, I promise."

"Okay," she said. But she wasn't convinced, and I knew it.

Don't be scared, I wanted to say to her. *Just don't ever be scared like I am.*

But I was too afraid to say anything. Too frightened of my own tears.

I un-muted the TV and escaped into the kitchen, where, in flagrant violation of the house rules, I dialed Richard's number.

"This is Laura," I said when he answered. "Could we just please talk?"

There was a pitying silence. "You got my email," he said. His voice was soft.

"I haven't checked my email," I said.

"Oh," he said. I could feel him shifting gears. "You should read it."

"What does it say, Richard?" I said. "I want to hear it from you."

A long sigh breathed its way through the line, carrying with it the dread I'd been feeling all day.

"It says I think you read more into our friendship than was actually there," he said. "I don't want to get as involved as you do—and it's not you. It's any girl."

"Then we won't get involved!" I said. "I'm fine with just being friends. I liked it the way it was. I thought YOU didn't!"

He was quiet again. His failure to take me at my word spoke volumes.

"You liked us being friends, didn't you?" I said.

"I did. At first." I could hear him switching the phone to his other ear and sighing miserably. "I wish you'd read my email. I explained it all."

"Y'know, I think I at least deserve to hear it straight from you," I said. My voice was teetering on the edge of those tears I'd been holding back, and I didn't try to stop them. "Why did you stop liking me?"

"I didn't stop liking you! See, that's just it. You're so intense. At first, I thought you were just, like, passionate, you know, about life and God, like I am. But then it just got so heavy. Like if I didn't call you or email you, you couldn't handle it. And then I couldn't follow my Bible verse—I didn't think what I was saying and thinking was acceptable to God anymore." I could tell he was swallowing hard. "I can't be somebody's whole life," he said. "Not even if I were married to them. GOD has to be your life."

The bride Laura in my vision suddenly turned and bolted down the aisle, her pearled train tripping her as she cried out in pain and tried to get to the church door, to get away from a rejection she couldn't stand.

"I hate saying this to you," he said. "I think you're still a cool girl, but I can't do this, y'know. Not like we were doing it."

"Then we'll do it another way."

"Laura—no. Not until—"

"Until what?"

Even as I grasped at the straw, I knew it wasn't really even there. I just let myself cry. Hard.

"I guess 'til you see that I'm not your answer," Richard said. "And see, that's why I said in my email that you should keep coming to church and youth group. I think Ethan can really help you. I don't think I should keep bringing you, but Anna and them will—"

"NO!" I said.

And then I threw the phone across the kitchen, pelting it straight into the refrigerator door where it hit with a plastic smack and scattered its every removable piece to the floor. In a sightless blur, I hurled myself into the family room and onto the couch. That was as far as I could get. The sobs coming out of me were paralyzing. I lay on my face, entirely at their mercy.

"Laurie?" said a little voice near my ear. "Laurie, do you need a blankie?"

"No, Bonnie!" I shouted into the couch cushions. "Just leave me alone for a minute. Just leave me alone!"

"Okay," she said.

Her voice was fragile and frightened, but I couldn't go to her. I couldn't do anything but sob myself down into the spiral that seemed to have no end.

You're nobody again, it hissed to me. *You're nobody—and you always will be.*

It kept hissing and hissing until it turned into gasping. And then I realized it wasn't that voice or even my own that was groping for air.

It was Bonnie.

I bolted up on the couch, searching frantically for her. She was on the floor, just below where my head had been, and she was choking in rattling heaves that were giving her no air. Her eyes were terrified.

"Bonnie!" I cried. "Bonnie, can you breathe, baby?"

She shook her head. The chubby hands flapped up and down in panic.

I tore for the kitchen and realized with horror that I'd rendered that phone inoperable. Screaming, "Hang on, Baby! Just hang on!" I flung myself down the hall to my parents' room and snatched up the bedside phone. With trembling fingers, I dialed 911.

chapter thirteen

It was like a long *déjà vu* nightmare.

There I was once again holding Bonnie and praying that she wouldn't die before the ambulance got there.

Watching helplessly as the paramedics plastered an oxygen cone over her face and wheeled her out on a stretcher.

Waiting endlessly in the emergency room for Mom and Dad to come out and tell me that yet again, I had endangered their baby's life, maybe even for good this time.

But I didn't give her anything she wasn't supposed to have! I kept telling myself. *Did she get into something when I was on the phone? Is that how I did it?*

It was Dad who came out with the news. His face looked ashen as he sat down beside me, rubbing his palm across his mouth.

"Is she okay?" I said. "Please tell me she's okay."

"She's not okay," Dad said. "But she's stabilized."

His words were stiff, as if he wished he'd had more rehearsal time before he delivered them to me.

"How is she not okay?" I said. "Is there going to be, like, brain damage or something?"

I'd considered every horrible possibility by then, and they were all waiting in line to convict me.

"No!" Dad said in his that-was-a-stupid-question voice. "There are just complications."

"I don't understand! I didn't give her anything she wasn't supposed to have, and I didn't leave anything out that she could have gotten into while I wasn't looking. I was only on the phone for—"

I stopped. My father had his hand on my arm.

"This wasn't an allergy attack," he said. "Bonnie has asthma. Severe asthma. It wasn't your fault this time."

I felt like I'd been backhanded in some way that was supposed to make me feel better. I tried to hone in on what was essential.

"Asthma?" I said. "She never had asthma before!"

"She's developed it. Possibly related to the allergies, they don't know."

Every statement my father was making sounded like he considered it the final word. But each one left me clawing for something that would make sense to me.

"But why now?" I said. "What brought it on all of a sudden?"

"They don't know, Laura," he said, less than patiently. "Could be something emotional. Could be some factor we don't know about."

"Something emotional?"

"Look," he said. His voice brought me sharply to a halt. "Don't start beating yourself up like your mother does. This could have happened when Bonnie was in school or when she was with me or Mom. It isn't your fault. You didn't do anything wrong. Period. End of discussion."

I started to cry—as if I'd ever actually stopped—and he sighed, put his arm around my shoulders, and patted me as if I'd merely failed to score the winning point on the athletic field.

"We're all upset about it," he said. "It's a serious illness and she's going to have to stay in the hospital probably for a couple of days at least. We just need you to stay focused and be supportive. Especially for your mother. She thinks this is all happening because she's working." Dad shook his head and attempted a smile. "You women. I don't know what I'm going to do with you."

He gave my arm another sound patting and went back to Bonnie and Mom with a promise to let me know as soon as I could see my sister. I was left with the very certain knowledge that this was NOT my mother's fault. It was all mine.

Decision: I was basically the most worthless person ever to walk the planet. I had wrecked my friendship with Celeste, ruined my relationship with Richard, and nearly destroyed my baby sister all together. God had listened and answered, and I'd blown it all.

The jury's verdict was clear. I was nobody.

And nobody was something I couldn't stand to be. I found myself revolting to be with. Mine was a disgusting skin to live in.

I certainly couldn't sleep with me, that night or any after that. While Mom stayed at the hospital and Dad worked half the night at his computer, I sat hunched like Quasimodo on my bed, pleading with the night to go away.

The days were no better. I couldn't eat. The very thought of food made me gag. I drank water by the gallon because my mouth was so dry my palate was sticking to my tongue. Despite all the fluids I was taking in, my lips cracked and dried out and bled every time they brushed against my braces. The view in the mirror was even uglier than usual. I scoffed at myself for ever feeling "a little bit cute."

I went to school on Friday because I had to, though I hid from Celeste and was grateful I didn't have Group and that Trent was still out with whatever injuries had been inflicted on him in the fight. Over the weekend, I tried to bury myself in homework, but I couldn't concentrate, and that sent the anxiety over the top. I had always, always been able to lose myself in work.

I tried spending time with Bonnie in the hospital, but they were keeping her sleepy, and whenever she was awake I was afraid that the mere sight of me would drive her to hysteria again and she would start gasping for air and maybe never find it this time . . .

Decision: I told Mom I thought I was getting a cold and that I probably shouldn't hang out in Bonnie's room. I opted for keeping the house clean, the laundry done, and meals cooked for Dad. At least I could do that without a lot of concentration.

The whole time I was scrubbing the grout on the kitchen counters with a toothbrush and folding the ends of the toilet paper just so on their rolls, I was ruminating, envisioning myself pushing Bonnie away because some jerk of a boy had just dumped me. As if I had ever expected him to have me in the first place. To think ahead was too frightening, so I just kept obsessing over the same ugly thoughts. By Sunday, I was praying for Monday and the welcome distraction of schoolwork.

Decision: I would throw myself into chemistry and prove that I could do at least something right.

But Trent still wasn't back on Monday, and on Tuesday, I asked Mr. Frohm if he knew how he was.

"His nose was broken," he told me. "That, and he's so shaken up by this whole thing he's afraid to leave his house." Mr. Frohm shook his bald head. "You kids act like there's a war on right here in the halls."

"I'm sorry," I said, for no apparent reason.

He gave me a knowing look, though what he knew I had no idea. "I'm going to give you Trent's number," he said "I think he'd appreciate a call from you."

I took it, but I didn't call. I was the last person who was going to cheer up somebody who was scared to death.

As long as I was in class, I could maintain the appearance that I wasn't losing my mind. As soon as there was any free time, though, I had to struggle to hold onto my sanity. The kind of thinking that no longer made sense, even to me, elbowed its way in the minute my mind wasn't focused on quadratic equations or *The Scarlet Letter.* You know you're in trouble when you prefer Nathaniel Hawthorne to your own thoughts.

Lunchtime was the worst. I missed Celeste, but I avoided her. I didn't want to actually HEAR her say we were through as friends now. I couldn't take it again.

Since eating was out of the question, I just sat at a table in the courtyard and stared into space, trying to stay numb. Celeste found me there on Wednesday. She sat herself across from me and looked straight into my eyes.

"All right," she said. "So Richard broke up with you. It's not the first time that ever happened to anybody. It's my fault you're this upset. I had you thinking he was about to propose."

"It's not your fault," I said.

She stared at me. Her smile spread slowly over her face. "Then you're not mad at me?"

I shook my head. "It's not your fault," I said again. "It's mine. I've just screwed everything up."

"What have you screwed up? It's not like you've had all this experience with guys. And Richard's not the only boy out there. You know I could hook you up with—"

"No," I said. "It wouldn't make any difference. It's not even about that."

Celeste studied me, as if she were trying to figure out what there could be besides boys for something to BE about. I wasn't sure I could even tell her.

"You look terrible," she said.

"Thanks," I said.

"No, I mean you're still gorgeous. You just look like you're sick."

"Sick of myself," I said.

"Would you knock it off? What is this all about, anyway?"

"I don't know! I'm just so scared, Celeste! I don't even know who I am anymore. I don't even feel like I have a self. I just keep thinking, heck, why don't I just kill myself."

Celeste's head snapped up at me. "You did not just say that."

"No, I didn't," I said. "I didn't say it."

"Yes, you did. You just said you ought to KILL yourself, Laura! What is up with that?"

"I didn't say it," I told her again. But I knew I had, and I wanted to say it again and again because it was now screaming in my head. Something I hadn't even known was there was now clawing and scratching at me and making my heart pound and my chest heave to get air and the whole courtyard spin, faster and faster into a blur.

"Dude, is she okay?" I heard a male voice say.

"No!" Celeste said. "Pick her up! We're going to Mrs. Isaacsen's."

"Dude, she needs the nurse!"

"No, just do it. Just bring her!"

I didn't fight any of it. I knew I was dying. I knew I didn't have to kill myself because I was already dying. Just dissolving into nobody at last.

I came back to life in a chair with a blanket around me and a cup of green-looking tea tucked between my hands and Celeste and her porter sent off with assurances that I was going to be fine.

"You got one messed-up friend," I heard the guy say.

"Shut up," Celeste said back.

And then it was quiet except for the ticking of the frog clock. I couldn't fight the silence anymore. I held my teacup and let it be.

"How you doin', sweetie?" Mrs. Isaacsen said.

"Horrible," I said.

"That's my girl. Following that honesty rule."

"I said I wanted to kill myself, but I really don't. It was like this voice in my head was taking over. I just can't think anymore." The anxiety began to rise again. "Am I going crazy?" I said.

"No," she said. "But your spirit is suffering. Can you eat?"

"No."

"Sleep?"

"No."

"Concentrate?"

I shook my head.

"How are the panic attacks?"

"How did you know about all this?"

"You're depressed, darlin'," she said. "Clinically depressed. You're feeling the same way you would feel if somebody had died." She smiled a little. "In a way somebody has."

"Who?"

"The old Laura Duffy. But this will go away, all of this, because the new Laura Duffy is about to be born. That is, if you'll let her come to life."

"I can't listen anymore! I get too scared when I listen!"

"I'm more concerned about this talk about killing yourself."

I shook my head, hard. "I don't really want to die! I just don't want to live like THIS!"

"And I don't blame you," Mrs. Isaacsen said. "Just let me ask you, have you done anything at all to hurt yourself? Have you cut yourself? Poked yourself with a paper clip?"

"No," I said.

"Have you thought about how you might kill yourself, mapped out any kind of plan?"

"No. All I've had is this voice thing that says, 'Why don't you just kill yourself?' It's like it isn't even me."

"It isn't," Mrs. Isaacsen said. "It's Evil whispering in your ear, because it knows how close you are to new life."

"Are you going to tell me to stay on this threshold thing?" I said. "Because I'll do whatever you say, but I can't stand where I am."

"No, absolutely not," she said. Her voice was firm and strong and it let me ease back a little in the chair. "Where YOU are is not a good place to be for too long. You're too open to sinister suggestions here, as you've seen. It's time to see the other side, Laura."

"Then please take me there," I said. "Please—I'll listen to you this time. I want a life."

"You're going to have one. You're going to have your authentic life. Now, let's take care of the physical part first."

Within a few minutes, she had me focusing on how much weight and sleep I'd lost and how I was going to get those back. She bypassed the Post-It Notes and went for a notepad with frogs on it, where she wrote down the daily schedule we devised together. There was a "grazing plan" since a whole plate of food made me feel like I was going to throw up, and a list of things to try if I couldn't doze off right away or if I woke up scared in the middle of the night. And there were directions for EXACTLY what I was supposed to do in my listening time.

"This isn't the whole answer," she said to me as she tore off the filled sheet and handed it to me. "But this will keep you calm and focused so you can open yourself up to God. You need some structure right now. Your poor little spirit is all over the place."

"I'm already not feeling so scared right now," I said.

She squeezed my hand. "That's good, that's what we want. But don't panic if you have another anxiety attack. Those aren't going to go away over night. Just pray your way through them, like we just talked about. Keep your psalms handy so you can pray those."

"So I can control it," I said.

"No, so you can manage it. The control is God's. You surrender to his control and he gives you the power to manage whatever happens."

She let that sink in before she leaned toward me again. "Now," she said, "you came in here in pretty bad shape just now." She glanced at her watch. "That's why we've been in here for two hours."

"No stinkin' way!"

"Yes, way, stinkin' or not. I think you ought to let me drive you home too."

"I'm okay, really."

"Right now you are, and I think you'll stay that way. But this is serious, Laura. You haven't actually entertained the thought of suicide, but you've let it in. If you even give it a place to sit down in a moment when you're not giving all the control to God, you'll be in trouble. I don't want you getting that low again."

"So what do I do?"

"The second you feel yourself going down into that spiral again and that voice even breathes its first syllable in your ear, you pray, and you pray, and you get yourself to someone and tell them what's going on. I don't care if it's the middle of the night and you have to call me. My home number is on that paper I just gave you."

"I could call you at home?" I said.

"The number is there. Now hear me, Laura." Her voice grew even more somber. "I think, right at this very moment, that I can help you through this. But you need to tell your parents, as well. Promise me you will do that, or I'm going to have to."

"They already have so much stress with Bonnie—"

"You're their daughter too. Do I have your word?"

"Okay," I said. My anxiety was whipping up just thinking about revealing this to my mother. I didn't even have to go as far as visualizing it.

From far away, a bell rang. Mrs. Isaacsen didn't move to get up. "One more thing," she said. "Like I said, I think I can be the one to help you through this. But if it looks like the situation requires more help, a psychologist maybe, I want you to try not to balk at that. God brings healing in a lot of different ways, and we have to surrender to that."

"And what if that doesn't work?" I said. "Will they put me in a mental hospital? Are we talking shock treatments and drugs and—"

Mrs. Isaacsen let rip with her wonderful laugh. "I don't think you're going to get anywhere close to a mental hospital," she said. "Or a psychiatrist's couch. If you can visualize all that, you're going to be able to SEE what God's doing in you. Besides—" She stood up, eyes twinkling, and pulled her purse out of her desk drawer. "You'd talk the ears off of any psychiatrist I've ever met. You'd have Sigmund Freud telling you to take a breath!"

"Do I really talk that much?" I said as we walked down the hall together. "I don't talk that much, do I? I mean, I know I think a lot, but does it all really come out of my mouth? I thought I was kind of quiet. Or maybe medium quiet—"

Mrs. Isaacsen laughed all the way to the car. When I gave her directions to the house, she sobered up a little.

"Who's going to be home when you get there?" she said.

"Nobody," I said. "My dad's at work and my mom's at the hospital with Bonnie. They're supposed to be letting her come home tomorrow."

"Hmm," Mrs. Isaacsen said. "I'm not sure you need to be alone yet. No point in inviting trouble, you know?"

I churned a little in the seat. And then I knew what I was supposed to do. It just came to me like a natural thought.

"Could you take me to the hospital, then?" I said. "Is that out of your way?"

"Not at all. I think that's a great idea. Then you can be with your family." She gave me a direct look. "And there IS something you need to tell them, right?"

"Yeah," I said. I was going to tell them about my suicide thoughts. But there was something else I had to tell them too.

Decision: No more secrets. Nothing anymore but honesty, no matter how bad the truth made me look.

And besides, how could I look any worse?

When I got up to the third floor where they had Bonnie, I was surprised to see my dad standing in the hall outside her door. The first thing that flashed through my mind was the certainty that she was worse and they'd called him from work . . .

I told myself to shut up and hurried up to him. When I said his name, he looked up at me as if I'd just caught him in a nap.

"What are you doing here?" he said, not unkindly.

"What are YOU doing here?" I said. "Why aren't you at work? Is she worse?"

"No, no, she's fine. They're sending her home tomorrow."

"Then why—"

"Because I want to be with my girls," he said.

I watched in sheer shock as tears shimmered over his eyes.

"I spend too much time at work," he said. "If there's an emotional element to Bonnie's illness, it's probably because I'm never there for her. Never there for you."

I was shaking my head.

"It's true," he said. "I know it is, and I'm going to try to make that up to you kids—"

"That's not the reason, Dad!" I said. "That's not the reason she had her asthma attack!"

I'd planned to approach this calmly, but somehow he'd sprung it on me, and the anxiety was pumping all over again. Maybe it was because now that I saw him so full of the love he hadn't shown in so long, I knew what I was going to lose when I told him the truth.

But I had to. I had to.

"Laura, I thought we discussed this—"

"But you don't know everything!" I said. "So just listen! That day, Richard broke up with me over the phone and I got hysterical and I was screaming on the couch and Bonnie tried to comfort me but I pushed her away and told her to leave me alone and the next thing I knew she couldn't even breathe. I was the reason she had an asthma attack, Dad, NOT you!"

And then, because I knew I couldn't stand the look that was about to come over his face, I turned around and ran down the hall. If he called after me, I didn't hear him. I didn't even take the chance of waiting for the elevator. I just tore blindly down three flights of stairs and through the lobby and out the revolving glass doors.

From there, I didn't know where to go. It didn't really matter, because what was I going to do when I got there? All I knew was

that I wanted to run away from the anxiety before it took me down
into that place I couldn't live in anymore.

So I just kept running. Into the Cove. Down to Bunker's Cove
Road. Away from the perfect houses and the Yacht Club and the
signs that shut me out. I kept going until the shoreline ran out of
room and there were no more houses and trees but only sidewalk
and benches and a railing. I ran until I realized that I was on the
Bay, that it was fifteen feet below me.

It was just a short climb away, over the railing, and I could drop
down into its deep, deep water.

I stopped, lungs hauling in air like I'd already been under the
water for as long as I could stand. I leaned against the railing, just
to catch my breath, and that's when I saw it.

The sky was a blaze of crimson and purple and passionate pink,
just as it had been that night on the Gulf, the first time I'd seen
God in glory like that. A wash of shame swept over me.

I had a chance to listen to you that night, God, I thought. *It could have
all gone in a whole other direction starting right then if I'd only listened.*

*Yeah, well, you blew it, so why don't you just throw yourself over this
railing and get it over with?*

It was more than a thought. It was a harsh whisper in my ear,
just as Mrs. Isaacsen had said it was. I had to tell someone. I had to
find somebody and tell them.

*And this would accomplish what? It isn't going to change anything. It
isn't going to bring Richard back. It isn't going to erase everybody's
memory of you having a breakdown in the courtyard. You think they
hung onto the Douglas Kunkle thing back home? You haven't heard
anything yet!*

My hands were clutching the railing so hard the metal was
cutting into my flesh. But I couldn't let go, or I knew I'd be over
the side so fast—

*You can't let go because you want to cut yourself. That's the first step.
Go on; see if you feel any pain.*

"No! God—no! Make it stop!"

I cried it out loud, and I pulled my hands away from the railing
and put them up to my mouth.

"I'm not going to kill myself!"

*Why not? What have you got to live for anyway? Your parents aren't
going to trust you now. Bonnie knows as well as you do that she almost
died because of you. And forget your little Crazy Group. Even Mrs.
Isaacsen said you needed a psychiatrist.*

"Make it stop, God!" I whispered. "Please make it stop!"

Throw your leg over that railing, girl. You're never going to get another chance like this. It's either this or the mental hospital.

Under me, my leg twitched, but I shook my head. Mrs. Isaacsen had said she didn't think that would happen.

She's a liar. She's nothing but a liar—

It was then that I snapped out the voice, just snapped it out with a toss of my head. My hair plastered itself against my face in the damp air and cars swished by behind me, and I knew I'd chased the voice away.

It was gone because it didn't know the truth that God himself had made crystal clear to me that day. It didn't know that Mrs. Isaacsen would never, ever lie to me.

Suddenly I was so tired I couldn't stand up anymore. I got myself to a bench and sat there, lapping up the sunset with my eyes until every streak dissolved peacefully into the almost dark.

There was no voice now, except my own.

I give up, God. Take control. Show me every life-making word You've got. I can't do this by myself anymore.

And probably—I never had been able to.

chapter fourteen

When the elevator doors slid back on the third floor, my parents were both standing outside Bonnie's door. I knew I was in for an ambush, but maybe I could manage it now. At least I had nothing left to lose by telling them about the suicide thing.

But before the doors even closed behind me, my mother was running toward me with her arms out. She pulled me into a hug so hard she knocked the air out of me.

"Mom, I'm sorry," I said.

"Oh, Laura, do shut up, honey."

Mom pushed me away from her but held onto me tight by the shoulders. People had to jockey around us to get down the hall, but she wasn't budging, and she wasn't letting go of me.

"Now you listen to me," she said. "No matter what happened that day, it is not your fault that Bonnie got sick. Do I have to make you repeat it after me, or are you going to believe it?"

I looked over her shoulder at Dad. He shrugged as if to say, *I*

TOLD you.

"You have always been far too hard on yourself, Laura," Mom said. "And don't either of you roll your eyes because I know where you get it. I'm the first one to admit it." She gave me a little shake. "Maybe you and I need to work on that together. I don't know if we need counseling—"

"I have a counselor," I said. "Mrs. Isaacsen at school. We talk about God and everything. And I KNOW I need her, Mom, because I was ready to kill myself. I mean, I thought about it."

The color drained simultaneously from their faces. Mom tightened her fingers so hard she was pinching my skin.

"I'm okay now," I said. "If I feel that again I'm supposed to go to you or somebody else—even if it's the middle of the night."

"Do we need to take you to a doctor?" Dad said.

"No, I'm okay. Honest."

"I'm calling your counselor," Mom said "No arguments."

"I have her home phone number," I said.

Mom pulled me back into her arms and held onto me so I could feel her silent tears.

"I'm sorry about Richard," she said. "Why didn't you tell me? You keep so much to yourself, Laura."

There's a really good reason for that, Mom, I thought. *And Dad. Let's see, there's the fact that you expect me to take on all the responsibilities of an adult, only I get none of the freedoms. You criticize everything I do that isn't perfect. You spring changes on me that I hate and then think I'm going to smile about it—*

They were both watching me. I had the perfect opportunity to dump all of that right on them, right at this moment when I had their full attention and sympathy.

But it felt like I ought to do something else first. Maybe pray. Talk to Mrs. Isaacsen. Get quiet with it.

I didn't know, and the not knowing made me anxious. It still wasn't entirely clear what I should do.

But I let it go. That's what she'd said to do. Just surrender it to God and he'd help me manage it.

I didn't exactly feel powerful. But I could still breathe. And I could follow my parents down to the cafeteria and eat some of the food that tasted like sawdust and match my mother sarcastic comment for sarcastic comment about it. And that night I could fall asleep at eight o'clock and sleep like a baby until morning.

The sleep alone made me feel like a different person. I was cautiously calm as I headed for my locker the next morning. The minute I saw it, though, calm went out the window.

The vine was back, and now it had tiny, delicate branches shooting out from it where the bulges had been before.

My first instinct was to look around for the janitor. If Mr. Clean saw this, I was going down.

But my next thought took over, and I squatted down in front of it. Once again, the clamor of the hallway faded behind me, and the vine itself pulled me in.

"Where did you come from?" I whispered to it. "Is there something you want to tell me?"

"Okay, so let me guess." It was the guy three lockers down. "You're doin' a science project on talkin' to plants."

I just kept smiling at my vine.

"Well, let me save you the trouble," he said. "My old lady yaks her head off at 'em and it don't work. Every plant that comes in our house dies."

"Whatever," I said. That word did come in handy now and then. I didn't know what else to say.

The first warning bell rang, and I shook myself back to reality and opened my locker. Another note dropped out.

It surprised me for a second. I'd forgotten about that part of it. The vine had kind of taken on a life of its own. I almost didn't want to think some guy had put it there. I'd basically had it with guys.

But I opened the note, written in the same perfect calligraphy, and read it:

> Hear me out.
> A Secret Admirer.

I whipped around to see if anybody were peeking at me from one of the corners or something, but everyone seemed to be bent on dragging out books and avoiding getting to first period any sooner than they had to. I stuck the note in my backpack with the other one. When I closed my locker door, my fingers lingered on my vine.

This day went a little faster than they had been going lately, maybe because I could concentrate a little better. I was even thinking I might get some homework done in the library during activity period, when I walked in and saw Trent at our usual table.

"Hey!" I said to him, as loudly as I dared with Mrs. Shush standing behind the counter. "You're back!"

He grinned sheepishly, and painfully, I was sure, what with his nose swollen to twice its original size and turned the color of a plum to boot. His eyes, however, gazed at me like a puppy's. Well, a puppy with bad contact lenses.

It hit me like a rock out of the little asparagus from Veggie Tales' slingshot.

Trent had a crush on me. And with his thing for science, the vine approach only made sense. He probably had some plant nutrition system going behind the locker walls.

I kept smiling as I sank into the chair across the table from him. It was okay that he was the Secret Admirer. I wasn't looking for a boyfriend anyway. Been there, done that.

But I definitely didn't want to lead Trent on, either. In a way, I felt like Richard did that to me, even though I was the one who had blown it. I didn't want anybody, especially a sweet guy like this, feeling the way I'd felt. The way I still felt sometimes.

Still, Trent had asked me to hear him out, and that I could do. I also wanted to know how he got that vine to stick on my locker door. And how he got it to practically speak to me . . .

"So talk to me, Trent," I half-whispered across the table. "I'm listening."

He reached for my chemistry book, but I pulled it back toward myself. "I don't mean that," I said. "Just tell me about—stuff."

I expected enough shuffling around to pull the carpet up, but to my surprise, he glanced warily at the librarian, moved to the chair next to me, and started in.

"I just stood there when they attacked me."

"Two guys with pierced chins?" I said. "What else were you supposed to do?"

"They jumped me from behind. I was just putting my laptop in my locker and they were just all of sudden there, taking me apart."

"There was nothing you could do in that situation."

He attempted a smile. "I could have hit them over the head with my computer." He grimaced. "If they hadn't already smashed it on the floor."

"No stinkin' way!"

"SHHHH!"

I turned and mouthed an "I'm sorry" at Mrs. Shush and scooted closer to Trent. "You were in shock," I whispered. "You can't do anything when you're in shock like that. It all happens too fast."

"That's fine if you're a girl. But guys are supposed to react. We're supposed to get ticked off and start swingin'." He shook his head.

"I just felt powerless. Man, I hate that feeling."

"You've been attacked before?"

"I get attacked around here all the time. Not like physically. Mentally. Verbally. I'm not like THEM, so the only time they leave me alone is when I'm in the lab or working with Mr. Frohm. Or—when I'm here doing this." He looked as if he were trying to retract his head into his shirt. "You're the only one I've talked to about this."

"What about Ponytail Boy?" I said.

"Who?"

"Your friend with the ponytail. Tall guy."

Trent shrugged. "Don't know anybody like that."

"He knows you. He was really concerned about you the day you got attacked."

"Whatever," Trent said.

I pushed that away, and with it the danger of leading him on. That was no longer part of the equation. I tore a piece of paper out of my chemistry notebook.

"I know exactly how you feel," I said. "Exactly. Here's my email address." I scrawled it across the paper. "Anytime you want to talk, just email me. I'll listen." I looked at him emphatically. "I'll always hear you out."

"Let me give you mine too," he said, without batting a contact lens. He tore a tiny scrap off of my paper and printed in tiny letters. His screen name was EINSTEIN. "That's what they call me in P.E." he said.

I nodded absently. I was studying his miniscule printing. It was barely legible. Certainly not calligraphy.

Of course, he could have had his mother write the notes.

Oh, come ON, I told myself. *He's not THAT much of a geek!*

And so, Trent and I became more than just student and tutor. We became friends. I liked my new connection with Trent, our emails and our talks, whether he was the Secret Admirer or not. In fact, I liked about an inch more of my life every day.

Some of my life was still pretty much laced around the edges with anxiety, and I still grieved on Wednesday and Saturday nights, and I wouldn't eat pizza on a Friday just on principle. When the school had a bonfire for basketball homecoming, around Thanksgiving, I almost didn't go, until Celeste made me dress up like a college preppie with her and drive to it with the top down on her car. It was hard to mourn the past when I was hanging out of a Mercedes wearing a cashmere sweater and pretending to drink from a Starbucks cup.

Even though the day after Thanksgiving started the biggest shopping season of the year and even though she had become practically an expert on bras and how they should fit, Mom quit her job in Dillard's bra department.

"What's to putting on a bra anyway?" Celeste said that night. We were painting my room a soft violet. "You wriggle yourself in there and you're good to go."

Dad, who was removing the crown molding from my ceiling, just grunted.

"There's a little more to it than that," Mom said. "But I'm going to let somebody else sell bras. I need to be at home."

I ignored the niggling little doubt that maybe she didn't really trust me with Bonnie anymore and said instead, "What about all the bills you wanted to pay off?"

"That doesn't have to happen in the next ten minutes," Mom said. "There are more important things than being debt-free."

"Like hanging out with us!" Celeste said.

"Yes, so you can eat me out of house and home." Mom picked up a plate heaped with sliced banana bread off the floor. "I want you to eat at least two pieces of this before you go to bed tonight," she said to me.

"I made her eat some of that lunch you packed Wednesday," Celeste said. "Gandhi ate more than she does."

"I'm doing better," I said. "I'm doing the grazing thing."

Mom didn't push it any further. She and I had had some long discussions about how hard it still was for me to eat sometimes when I was really nervous. She'd told me she wished she had my problem. When she got depressed, all she wanted to do was eat everything that wasn't nailed down. Somehow, it had been reassuring to me to find out that she'd lived with depression too. It was like we shared an experience and we could help each other.

She also said she wished she'd had a Mrs. Isaacsen in her life. I thanked God every single day that I did.

I went in to see Mrs. Iaascsen as often as I could, when she wasn't counseling somebody and I wasn't studying chemistry with Deidre during study hall. Deidre was a teacher's aide that period, so whenever there was nothing for her to do, she came to Coma Town and we balanced chemical reactions and wrote notes back and forth about the clowns in there. We gave them names like "Bozo" and "Ronald" and "Chuckles."

"We could write a play about them," Deidre said "A musical."

"You write music?" I said.

"I try," she said. "I'm taking music theory this semester."

"No stinkin' way!" I said.

I launched into a long explanation of my musical experiences. It was the first time I'd talked about Missouri in weeks. I started to feel wistful again, not for "home" but for singing and auditions and all the rest of it that was in my soul.

"Have you met Mr. Howitch?" she said.

"Is that the choir teacher?" I said. "No. I will next semester because I'll be in music theory—"

"No, you have to meet him now. I'll take you down there one day, like after school. You have to meet him."

Beside us, a lump on a desk stirred and "Bozo" lifted his head to squint at us.

"Do you mind?" he said. "People are tryin' to sleep here."

"Get a room," I said.

It was okay that I didn't get to talk to Mrs. Isaacsen everyday. There was something about knowing she was praying for me that made me feel a unique bond with her. I didn't have to be with her physically to feel that.

On the days when I did get to spend time with her in her office, I couldn't get enough of the things we talked about.

First, I'd report in about how I was eating and sleeping and managing the anxiety when it started to buzz. What she'd suggested to me was working. I was no longer sleeping with the TV on, and sometimes I didn't even turn on music because I was calm enough just listening, period.

"You oughta be teaching this stuff for a living," I teased her one day.

"Nah, nobody would ever pay me to do this," she said. "Besides, it's not me that's teaching you. Now, what about those holy moments of praise? Did you read Mary's Magnificat?"

"Yeah, and I read about Hannah. I even looked up Sarah and Rachel and a bunch of other women to see if they had them."

Mrs. Isaacsen looked at me over the tops of her half-glasses.

"I know, I'm not supposed to study, I'm supposed to listen," I said. "But I can't help it. I get on a roll."

"And what about Laura? Has she had holy moments of praise?"

"Yes. Like almost every time I go down to my bench."

The bench on the Bay had become my quiet place of choice. I put Celeste and Deidre off at least a couple of times a week and went down there by myself to listen. I was finding out that people didn't know how to be quiet anymore. They talked, like, constantly, as if they knew every single thing and had to tell the entire population of Panama Beach about it. But I was also finding out how to shut it out and hear instead the gawky cries of the pelicans, and the mutterings of the seagulls who sat puffed up on the railing observing me, and the whispers of God on the breeze.

I could actually just listen now, because Mrs. Isaacsen taught me what to DO instead of just sitting there and letting myself go nuts. Actually, she didn't teach me, I heard it in Psalm 34, which she suggested I listen to.

Now I blessed him and I breathed him and I smiled at him— which sometimes drew the curious stares of tourists passing by. If that didn't get them, me opening my mouth to TASTE him did. There was God in the salt air—and in my mother's pecan Christmas cookies. When I told Bonnie that, she started calling them God cookies. That's when Mom suggested to Dad that we find ourselves a church.

Celeste, with a mouth full of cookie, said, "Then I'm comin' too, Duffy." She almost never called me anything else after that.

"Have a lust for life," the Psalm said. "Be anxious every day to come upon beauty."

"I think I'm getting this lust thing down," I told Mrs. Isaacsen one day.

"Be careful who you say that to," she said, laughing. Then she suddenly reached over and hugged me. "Oh, Laura Duffy," she said, "you are starting to live a life that will always lift you above the mundane. Thank you for letting me watch it happen."

I wasn't sure whether it was actually HAPPENING, but I was understanding it better. I was seeing surrender in sailboats when they gave up control to the wind, and in seagulls when they caught a current and left the rest up to the air. But as far as getting it into my own life, I didn't know if I was doing that or not. Mrs. Isaacsen said maybe I ought to try taking a chance on something I couldn't possibly control myself and see what happened. I wasn't sure what that could be, until a couple of days later, when Deidre burst into chemistry and practically hurdled over two desks to get to me.

"You have to come with me to meet Mr. Howitch TODAY!" she said.

"Why?"

"Because he has to hear you sing. Somebody dropped out of the chorus and we start rehearsals right after Christmas."

"Chorus of what?"

"*Grease!* If he hears you sing, you are SO in." She narrowed her eyes at me from behind her glasses. "And don't give me any of that 'No stinkin' way' garbage. You're coming down there with me right after school."

Talk about surrender. She'd have dragged me down there if I hadn't acquiesced.

As it was, she pulled me by the hand over to Building 20 that afternoon—a very sweaty hand. I felt like I was sucking on cotton balls.

"Stop stressing," she said. "I've heard you sing. You're better than the girl playing Sandy, for Pete's sake." She looked at me sideways through a panel of red hair. "Maybe we could arrange an appendectomy for her or something."

It helped that Mr. Howitch was small, cute, and funny, and he didn't act like I was trying to strut in and take over his music department.

"Deidre thinks you're the next Celine Dion," he said from his birdlike perch on a high stool.

"No, I'm not!" I said. "I'm not quite that good!"

"Nobody expects you to be." He grinned through his little mustache and said, "Just sing like Laura. That's all I want you to do."

"What do you want me to sing?"

"Whatever you know." He moseyed over to the piano. " I can probably fake it."

"Um, 'Amazing Grace'?"

It wasn't exactly a show tune, but it was all I could think of at the moment, and besides, he wouldn't expect me to sing THAT like Celine Dion. He immediately played me an intro and paused for me to come in.

The first few notes were breathy. It had been a long time since I'd sung in front of anybody. But Deidre was sitting there in front of me, nodding like one of those dashboard dogs with springs for necks.

And I could almost hear Mrs. Isaacsen saying; *Make it a holy moment of praise.*

Thoughts like, *What about breath control? Do I have the high range today? Phrasing, do the phrasing,* all swept through my mind. And out again. Because once I was into the second measure, there was no turning back. I could either let myself sing the song, or I could mess it up by thinking too much.

And I WAS singing. And it was a God-song. I let myself sing until it was singing me.

Whether I got the part or not, it was the best I'd ever done.

"Why aren't you in my program?" Mr. Howitch said.

"Because I enrolled too late and all your groups were full."

"Who told you that nonsense?" he said.

"Dr. Vaughn—"

"From now on you come to me, now, y'hear?" he said, thrusting a thumb toward his chest.

"I hear," I said.

He smiled at me and shook my hand, as if he expected us to leave.

"Uh, Mr. Howitch?" Deidre said. "Is she in the chorus for *Grease* or what?"

"Well, duh," he said. He rolled his eyes dramatically. "Rehearsals start January third. Clear your calendar, girl."

I was sure he could hear the two of us screaming all the way out of Building 20.

The next day in Group, Celeste nudged me and said, "Tell 'em what happened yesterday."

"Is it okay?" I said to Mrs. Isaacsen.

"Of course. We want to hear each other's good stories, too."

With some goading from Celeste, I told them about doing the audition and getting into *Grease*. I didn't want to sound like I was bragging.

When I was through, Michelle was staring at me.

"So let me get this straight," she said. "You just went down there and started singing for this man."

"Yeah. It's what I do. I sing. It's my thing."

"Do you know who this guy is, though?" K.J. said. "He, like, wins awards for our choirs and musicals and stuff. Nobody gets into his program if they aren't, like, super good."

"Oh," I said.

"You don't believe me. Tell her, Miz I."

"Panama Beach IS known for its fine arts programs," she said.

"Kids transfer in here from other schools to get into his choirs," Michelle said, as if I wouldn't get the point unless she drilled it into my head. "I wanna know how you had the nerve to do that. I mean, no offense, but you're pretty much non-aggressive."

I looked at Mrs. Isaacsen. She nodded at me.

"I surrendered," I said.

"To what?" Michelle said.

They were all waiting for my answer.

"To God," I said. "I didn't have any control over how it came out, so I gave it to God and managed what he gave me and that's all."

"And that's supposed to work for me?"

We turned to look at Joy Beth. She was flipping her hair back over her shoulders like she was trying to kill it, and her chin was coming up so hard she could have chopped wood with it. I found myself shrinking back in my chair.

"Laura is just telling her story," Mrs. Isaacsen said to her. "If her faith is part of her story, she can talk about it. No one's trying to push it on you—"

"I didn't say she was tryin' to push it on me," Joy Beth said. She was straining like a horse eager to race. "I'd swallow the whole thing if I thought it would work for me. But it WON'T. I could make it to the Olympics but—"

"Haven't we heard all this before?" K.J. said. "I'm not trying to be mean or anything, but you won't tell us WHY your parents made you quit the swim team—"

"Because I'm a diabetic! My parents made me quit because I can't get my blood sugar under control. I might never get to compete on ANY level. I might go blind. I might end up with kidney failure." Joy Beth turned on me like a lioness. "Where was GOD when I got stuck with THIS disease?" she said.

She was breathing so hard I was afraid she was going to pass out. I looked helplessly at Mrs. Isaacsen. Was there something I was supposed to be able to say to her at this point? Something to make this okay? "Surrender," did seem pretty weak.

"You okay, J.B.?" Mrs. Isaacsen said.

"Yeah. I'm fine. Go on to somebody else."

We managed to pick up some kind of discussion again, but I couldn't help stealing looks at Joy Beth. She didn't LOOK out of control, but I could feel the panic that was coursing through her veins.

God, what do you say to somebody in a situation like this? I thought.

Since God wasn't forthcoming with an answer, I asked Mrs. Isaacsen about it that afternoon when we were drinking chamomile in her office after school.

"You can say this to her when the timing is right," she said to me. "Right now she's liable to deck you. Suffering is probably the most efficient means of transformation, and God makes full use of it whenever he can."

"Is that what God did with me?" I said. "I mean, I didn't have a disease—"

"But you were suffering. Sometimes you still suffer. You'll suffer again. We all will. What we have to help people to realize is that we shouldn't try to get rid of the pain until we've learned what the pain has to teach us."

"Can you show her that without talking about God?" I said.

"Good question, Laura," she said. "It's made me consider leaving the public school system more than once."

"No!" I said. "We love you!"

She gave me a misty smile. "That's why I'm still here, darlin'. Do you realize that you now have your first Secret Power?"

I thought for a moment before I nodded. "The Power of Surrender."

I breathed the words out more than said them. She sat in silence with me as they reached the air. It was a God-Wonder, I knew.

"Now," she said, "power doesn't come without responsibility. Once you begin to live the secret, you can't keep it a secret anymore. You have to share it."

I envisioned myself standing up on a table in the courtyard during lunch, holding forth, and it made me squirm in the chair.

"Don't go there, Laura," she said. "Relax. I have some Scripture for you to listen to."

How did she do that? How did she always know what I was thinking practically before I even thought it?

I waited for her to scribble some psalm numbers out on a Post-It Note, but she handed me a sheet with verses already typed out on it.

"This one really needs be read in the King James because it's so beautiful," she said. "I wasn't sure if you had one at home so I printed it out for you."

It said at the top of the page:

> *John 15:1-8*
> *I am the true vine, and my Father is the husbandman.*
> *Every branch in me that beareth not fruit He taketh away: and every branch that beareth fruit, He purgeth it, that it may bring forth more fruit.*
> *Now ye are clean through the word which I have spoken unto you.*
> *Abide in me, and I in you. As the branch cannot bear fruit of itself, except it abide in the vine . . .*

I stopped reading and stared up at her.

Mrs. Isaacsen was my Secret Admirer?

chapter fifteen

" I know the King James can be hard to get used to," Mrs. Isaacsen said. "But just listen to it—"

"It's not that."

I tried to stare her down, but she just looked back at me, her brow furrowed.

"Do you do calligraphy?" I said.

She laughed. "You've lost me, Laura."

"Never mind," I said.

I needed some time to sort this one through, and I was already sifting before I even got out of her office.

It couldn't be a coincidence, I thought as I headed for the locker hall, *her just giving me Scripture about vines and branches after what kept showing up on my locker door.*

And she couldn't be giving me the Scripture BECAUSE of the locker incidents. I'd never told her about them. The only people who knew about them were Celeste and Deidre, and I'd never shared the part about the notes with Deidre.

The notes.

I slowed to a crawl with the bank of lockers in sight.

It was one thing for Mrs. Isaacsen to put a vine on my locker to make a point. But to leave me a note from a "Secret Admirer" was like messing with my head. She knew how hurt I was by Richard. Would she really set me up to think some other guy was checking me out?

It seemed almost cruel, and I couldn't imagine my Mrs. Isaacsen being cruel.

I was so up-to-my-eyebrows in sorting as I rounded the last corner that I didn't see what was waiting for me until I was almost on top of it.

My entire locker door was covered with vine and branches—and lush bunches of ripened grapes, shining purple against gray metal.

I froze and put my hand over my mouth. I was still standing there when I heard Mrs. Isaacsen's voice behind me.

"Oh, good, I caught you. I forgot to give you the most important thing." She stopped at my elbow, and I heard her take in a sharp breath. "What's all this?"

Nice try.

"I know, Mrs. Isaacsen," I said. My voice sounded heavy.

"You know what, darlin?" She was still staring at my mini-vine-yard.

"You just came to see how I was going to react."

"I just came to give you something I want you to have. You rushed out of there so fast I nearly forgot."

She opened her hand and revealed a sterling silver bracelet, curled and shimmering in her palm.

My heart lifted a little. This, I thought, THIS was vintage Mrs. Isaacsen, not some convoluted plot to make me think I was being sought by a secret admirer who had a thing for produce. But I was so confused—

"Go ahead," she said. "It's for you."

It really was exquisite. Tiny links of silver tumbled one upon the other in a chain so dainty I was afraid it would dissolve between my fingers if I picked it up. It only took one more nod from her, though, for me to open my palm and let her slide it into my hand. As it fell like air across the tips of my fingers, a silver key no bigger than my thumbnail dangled from one of its links.

"You've discovered the key to one of your secret powers," Mrs. Isaacsen said. "Just by listening."

"It's beautiful," I said.

"Shall I help you put it on?" she said.

I just nodded, because I still wasn't sure WHAT was going on. She circled my wrist with the bracelet and snapped its tiny clasp in place. It shimmered against my skin. Mrs. Isaacsen held the charm against her fingertip.

"Now that you have the key," she said, "you can use it to unlock doors for yourself. You've already started to do that."

"They were ALL locked when I got here," I said.

"But—and this is what I was talking about when I said you can't keep the secret to yourself—make sure that when you open those doors, you let other people through as well."

Her eyes were flashing their passion, and she was speaking in that voice that warmed me right into belief. As tiny and graceful as it was, the bracelet felt as if it were glowing at my wrist, and sending its power straight to my soul.

And then Mrs. Isaacsen chuckled. "Now, darlin'," she said, "you want to tell me what this is all about?"

She nodded toward my locker.

"You really don't know?" I said.

"I'm completely mystified."

I folded the fingers of my other hand over the bracelet. One last test. Because I had to know.

"What do you want to bet there's a note?" I said.

As I squatted down and twirled my lock, I felt totally schizo: half of me wanting to believe she wasn't the phantom vineyard keeper, the other half convinced it couldn't be anybody else. Who else thought in symbols the way she did?

I pulled open the door, and the inevitable piece of white folded vellum tumbled out. I could feel Mrs. Isaacsen watching me from above as I slowly and carefully unfolded it.

In the accustomed calligraphy it said:

Relish the fruit. I love to see you in joy. —A Secret Admirer.

I stood up and handed it to Mrs. Isaacsen. Her eyebrows went up into their points and stayed there.

"This isn't the first one of these you've received?" she said.

"No. This is the third. Every time I get one, I cut the vine off, and every time, it comes back bigger."

I was still searching her face. Her eyes were confused.

And you thought I was doing it?" she said.

"Not 'til today when you gave me that Scripture." I shook my head hopefully as I spoke. "But you didn't do it, did you?"

She took my hand and tucked the note into my palm. The key dangled nearby.

"I admire you, Laura," she said. "But I've made no secret of it. No, this is some cute fella who's got it bad for you."

I let the air rush out of me. What the heck had I been thinking? This lady was all about honesty. She was the most authentic person I'd ever known.

Decision: I wanted to BE Mrs. Isaacsen when I grew up. Okay, so maybe the Laura version of authenticity.

I looked down to see her leaning over, running her fingers over the grapes. She was as enchanted as I was, and I sagged with relief.

"I think this is a beautiful thing," she said. "But—"

"I know," I said. "I gotta cut it off of here before Mr. Clean— before the janitor sees it."

"It isn't that." She straightened up to give me a somber look. "You don't feel like someone's stalking you, do you?"

"No! Do you?"

She looked back at the vine. "No," she said. "I'm just very protective of my chicks." She smiled at me. "Do you need a ride home?"

"No," I said. "I'm gonna stay here and try to get this off."

She patted my shoulder. "I'll see you tomorrow, then," and left.

Kneeling in front of my mini-vineyard, right in the middle of a hall that smelled like damp Nikes and echoed the complaints and curses of teenagers, this was suddenly a quiet place. I listened, and I heard the words in my head.

I am the vine, ye are the branches. He that abideth in me, and I in him, the same bringeth forth much fruit: for without me, ye can do nothing.

I glanced down at the paper, still tucked in my hand.

Relish the fruit.

There was only one thing to do then, as far as I could see. I tugged a grape from amidst the curly tendrils and popped it into my mouth. It burst in sweetness against my tongue, and I felt what it was to relish. I felt me as well, just being. Just being there with God who is sheer being itself. Just being there and tasting him. It was a knowing I couldn't explain. And I didn't try.

As I reached my hand out to take a second grape, I felt another presence. This one wasn't quiet, and it made me jerk my head around with the anxiety already flickering.

Shayla was standing above me.

Before I could even get to my feet, she had me by the front of my shirt, fingers clutching the cloth like wire claws. For a second her long, hard face was nearly pressed against mine as she pulled me toward her and then thrust me away. I flopped like a gym sock into a corner, where she reached me in one slicing stride and once again gathered my shirt front into her fingers and lifted me up and against the metal where two banks of lockers met. A fingernail nicked my flesh right through my blouse. And this time, her face, elongated by rage, stayed inches from mine.

"Don't open your mouth," she said. She was barely opening hers. Her words spat themselves out between her teeth like tiny pieces of gravel from her throat. "You just listen to me."

There wasn't much else I could do, and I knew it. My head was crammed into the metal corner. I couldn't even nod.

"You," she said. "YOU are the reason I'm doin' time right now. You and your whiney little, 'She hurt me. She pushed me.'"

I could feel my eyes springing wider. She did sound surprisingly like the Laura Duffy who had flung herself on the mercy of Mr. Stennis in the office that day. It seemed like a lifetime ago now.

"You didn't attack me in self-defense," she said. "They think you're this perfect little angel." Her hard mouth split into an ugly smile. "And I'm here to tear off your wings."

To my surprise, she let go and she stepped back from me. I was still cornered, though, and all I could do was look at her as she held out her arms, bent at the elbows, and beckoned me with her fingers. Nails the size of steak knives glinted under the overhead lights.

"Come on, New Girl," Shayla said. "Let's see what you can do without your weapon."

I stared, uncomprehending.

"Let's go! Let's finish this off!"

Slowly it dawned on me, and slowly I shook my head. "I'm not going to fight you," I said.

Her nails were on me like switchblades, stabbing into my arms as she snatched me up again.

"No?" she said.

"No, I—"

"Then just stand there and let me take you down!"

All I could do was squeeze my eyes shut and wait in terror that knocked me back like a body slam.

Except that it wasn't just terror. It was Shayla, lurching against me and then jerking away, as if she were being seized by some unseen force. But I saw it, and it was Joy Beth.

As I watched her yank Shayla's arms behind her as if she were going to tie them in a knot, and heard the swearing spewing from both of them like snake venom, my fear left, just walked away from the scene, dusted off its feet, and left the situation in Joy Beth's hands.

Hands that jerked Shayla up and rendered her helpless.

Except for her mouth. Shayla spat out words I'd never heard before, at least not in those combinations. When she'd used them all up, she stood there in Joy Beth's vice grip, breathing at me with nostrils flared so wide, Celeste could have driven her Mercedes through them.

"What do you want me to do with her, Duffy?" Joy Beth said. They were the first non-profane words she'd uttered since she'd arrived. "I'll do whatever you want."

"Like you could!" Shayla said.

"Shut up!" Joy Beth said.

Miraculously, Shayla did.

I had the absurd urge to laugh. Joy Beth looked anything but sickly, standing there with a girl as big as she was pinned to her. It was easy to envision J.B. demonstrating a wrestling smackdown move with Shayla, right there in the hall. I could see her body flopping like a caught flounder—

But it was just a silly picture, and not one I wanted to view. It suddenly struck me that I was feeling no anger, no desire to grab my backpack and inflict brain damage on Shayla. Seeing her there, seething and frustrated and powerless, I felt sorry for her.

"Let's listen to her," I said to Joy Beth. "See what she has to say."

Joy Beth looked less than impressed with that choice, but she tightened her grip on Shayla and said, "Okay. So talk."

For a second or two, Shayla couldn't seem to think of anything to say. The words that followed that momentary lapse blued the air.

"Quit cussin'," Joy Beth said, giving Shayla a shake. "She's a Christian."

"And I care about that because—?"

"Start talkin'."

"What's the point?" Shayla said. "I talked to her before, told her not to tell that she saw me and that black chick fightin'. And did she listen?" Shayla snorted. "So now I'm in Juvie—but I've been a good girl and got out on a pass. Just long enough to come and find

YOU."

She tried to lunge toward me, but Joy Beth had her so locked up, her move was barely a hiccup.

"You're a moron," Joy Beth said to her. I could almost feel her hot breath on Shayla's ear. "In the first place, you were hauled in for suspected fighting so many times, it was only a matter of time before they nailed you. What—you think you can go around slammin' people into lockers and not get caught?"

Shayla answered with a grunt. Her eyes were riveted on me. By now, I had peeled myself out of the corner and was leaning with my arms folded against someone's locker. As I looked back at her, she seemed to be shrinking right in Joy Beth's arms.

"Oh, and let me clear somethin' up," Joy Beth said. "They don't give passes in Juvie. So you're even more of a moron for breaking out and coming here because they're gonna find you and drag your tail right back there and you'll do double time."

"Like you know anything about Juvie," Shayla said. She gave that derisive hiss that had practically sacred the pee out of me the first day I'd seen her. Now it was merely like air going out of a shriveling tire.

"I know about Juvie," Joy Beth said, "because I been there. Before I got sense, which is what you oughta do."

"Did you get Jesus, too?" she said. The way she said the name made me wince. "Yeah, that solves everything. You don't know nothin' about my life. A little prayer meetin' isn't gonna change MY life."

Joy Beth looked at me. "Aren't you gonna tell her?"

"Tell her what?" I said.

"Tell her to surrender."

Shayla let out a hoot. "Do I have a choice?"

"You got zero choices left, girlfriend."

All three of us whipped around as Mr. SRO appeared at the end of the hall. He strolled toward us, seeming perfectly confident that Joy Beth was going to keep Shayla in custody until he got there. He was shaking his head atop that thick neck.

"Girl," he said to Shayla when he reached her. "What part of this makes sense to you?"

"Nothin'," Shayla said. "Nothin' makes sense to me."

It was a shriveled, shrunken woman-child that Joy Beth turned over to Mr. SRO. Shayla let him snap the handcuffs on her and lead her down the hall, a mere raisin-version of her former self.

Joy Beth and I trailed behind, at Mr. SRO's request, so once again

I could give my eye witness account.

"This is becoming like a new career for me," I said.

"No stinkin' way," Joy Beth said.

I looked up at her, towering beside me like a protective shield. "Now YOU'RE saying it. Celeste is turning us all into New Yorkers."

"You're not a fighter," Joy Beth said. "So don't quit your day job or nothin'." She flipped her lanky blonde-ish hair over her shoulder—that shoulder that made me feel like I had a bodyguard. "It's just a good thing your friend told me you were in trouble."

"Huh?" I said.

"That guy. Long ponytail. I don't think he goes here. I'm coming out of the gym and he's standin' there and he says, 'I think that Duffy girl's got a problem down at the lockers.'" She shrugged the swimmer-shoulders. "What I don't get is why he didn't come down here himself. Anyway, whatever—the thing is, you can't deal with chicks like Shayla by standin' around listenin' to 'em talk."

I grinned at her. "We just did, didn't we?"

"Yeah, but—"

"We listened long enough for help to come along. If you'd beaten her up, you'd be in trouble. You'd be back in Juvie."

"Don't tell people I was ever in, okay?" she said. Her eyes flickered little points of fear.

"No stinkin' way," I said. "It's a secret."

We walked along in comfortable silence then.

Was she talking about Ponytail Boy? I thought. *How does HE know my name?*

The same way he knew Trent's probably. But it didn't feel weird or creepy. And I didn't feel the urge to go find him. I just felt the bracelet tickling my wrist, its tiny key brushing my skin in fine and fleeting little touches.

Decision: I'll keep your secret, Joy Beth.

And I'll let you in on one of mine.